# THE KALEIDOSCOPE JAGUARS OF THE JUNGLES OF MEXICATL

## AND OTHER STORIES

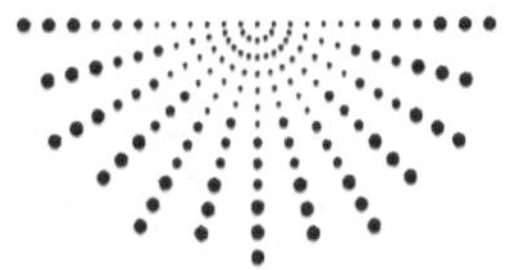

## STEPHANNIE TALLENT

For more information, contact: stephannie@stephannietallent.com

First e-Book edition November 2021

ebook ISBN: 978-1-942655-31-2
Print ISBN: 978-1-942655-32-9

www.stephannietallent.com

*To Juliet: Here's to more girls' writing weekends!*

# CONTENTS

# INTRODUCTION

Welcome to my ninth collection of short stories! Like **The Monkey's Journal**, this collection is primary fantasy, but the stories are perhaps a bit more eclectic.

*The Kaleidoscope Jaguars of the Jungles of Mexicatl* and *The Wretched Sunlight of Shasta* follow a self-described low-level sorceress to different worlds. I've included a bonus snippet of travel preparations prior to *The Kaleidoscope Jaguars* at the end of this collection.

*Crate Training* is a a piece of werewolf flash fiction that I entered into a contest. It didn't win the reader's choice that week, but the website editors did choose to include it in their yearly collection. It's cute and, well, biting.

*The Body Mage's Foot*, an alternate world fantasy, is just plain weird. Borders on light body horror. If you're squeamish, skip this one. Or you'll never look at meatballs the same way again.

*Blood Tracks* explores one young woman's experience with genome-changing nanobytes. I really like Bettina—I hope I'll be "seeing" and writing more of her story.

*The Girl Who Created a Mechanico Menagerie* is based on one of my favorite fairy tales, *The Boy Who Drew Cats*, and is an alternate world fantasy as well.

Enjoy!

# THE KALEIDOSCOPE JAGUARS OF
# THE JUNGLES OF MEXICATL

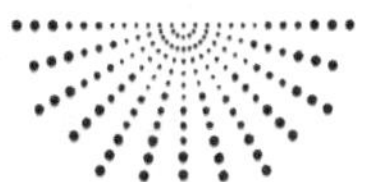

J acie laid flat on her belly along the fig tree branch that arced over the shallowest part of the stream, feeling the bumps and whorls of the thick branch through her chambray shirt and fitted black t-shirt.

Her long, silky black hair was pulled back in a thick braid that did nothing to cool her neck in the wretched heat. Every time she went into the field, she realized again she should cut it, but she couldn't bring herself to that. Her hair was her best feature. Her brown eyes were nice enough, her tall, lanky athletic figure acceptable, but her hair was glorious.

Stupid, but there it was.

She took a deep breath of the thick, humid air, and crinkled her nose. She smelled like a citronella candle, doused in insect repellant. The warm, compost-y smell of the jungle floor barely permeated the harsh lemon scent.

She wore an anti-vermin charm as well, a small bronze medallion on a black silk cord around her neck. Despite the magic-saturated atmosphere of Mexicatl, the local bloodsucking mosquitoes and ticks totally ignored the charm.

Apparently she was delicious.

She looked like she had chicken pox, from all the mosquito bites on her arms and legs. The little fiends feasted on her despite her loose-fitting camo pants and her long-sleeved cotton chambray shirt, buttoned up to her neck and sleeves rolled down.

Maybe if she was able to make her own charms, they would've worked better.

She couldn't make charms. She had no powers of divination, or healing, or luck. She was so terrible at offensive magics she didn't even practice anymore. One small offensive push took so much out of her she was flat on her back for a day. A big one might kill her.

*Her* talent lay in crossing over to different worlds.

She had tried going without bug spray, knowing the stench to be unnatural, but gave up. Too much risk of too many insect-borne diseases. If she caught something, who knew if it could be cured or even treated when they got back to their world.

And she itched. Gods above and below, she itched.

She checked her watch. 5 p.m. Not long before twilight. In the dense jungle, even perched up above the stream, the sunlight was filtered and dim the whole day, but the show started when the sun went down.

Dr Dani Blackblood napped above her, her small, wiry form tucked into a fork of two smooth branches, the brim of her ridiculous floppy hat pulled tight over her gray-streaked brown pixie cut, protecting her freckled face. The bugs didn't give a hoot about her. So unfair. Dani slept peacefully. She didn't even twitch despite the squawks and screeches of the violet and orange macaws swooping amongst the branches, or the occasional Tyrannosaurus-like roar of a howler monkey.

The canvas strap of the air rifle was looped over Dani's neck, the rifle snugged up against her body. Loaded sedative darts filled a case attached to her belt. Jacie knew, napping or not, Dani would be ready to go in three seconds if Jacie saw their target.

A kaleidoscope jaguar cub.

Deanna Montrose, a forty year old socialite from Dallas, Texas, rich with oil money from despoiling the Gulf of Mexico, had somehow heard of these cats, living in the jungles of Mexicatl, four worlds away from their own.

And she wanted one.

Jacie didn't know specifically how Montrose had found her. That was normal. Clients found her by quiet word of mouth: from oddball Reddit threads, from dark web chat rooms, from surreptitious conversations at fundraisers held by American old money royalty.

With her skill at world crossing, Jacie had created a career out of visiting nearby worlds and collecting critters for the highest bidder.

Dr Dani Blackblood, her best friend, was part of the package. A semi-retired veterinary anesthesiologist from Austin, Texas, with no magic of her own, Dani was Jacie's ace in the hole for safely delivering the animals across the worlds to their new homes.

Dani had helped on trips in the past. Baby triceratop-like dinos from northern Mexicatl, where millions of years ago the meteor had missed but the super volcanoes had still erupted? Check. Fuzzy gray dire wolf pups from way up north in Kanata, just two worlds away and still stuck in an ice age? Ditto. And dozens of other trips.

(Once the first season Game of Thrones came out on HBO, there was a run on dire wolf puppies. Jacie flat out detested snow. Those pups cost their buyers a pretty penny plus some.)

Sweat dripping down her neck and between her breasts, Jacie decided she hated heat and humidity as well.

———

WHEN THEY FIRST ARRIVED, searching out the best place to set up to catch a jaguar, Jacie and Dani took a trail that dead-ended into a muddy river that emptied out into the ocean, just a few hundred yards west. Water sources were always a good starting point, so they settled in to observe for a while.

They watched a deer try to cross the twenty-yard wide river. Fins sliced through the water towards the deer once the deer started swimming. Midway through its crossing, the deer had been yanked underwater and didn't resurface.

In Central America, in their world, bull sharks would swim into the rivers.

It looked like the same thing happened here.

If not bull sharks, something else that was hungry.

At night, they had also seen crocodiles, red eyes gleaming in flash-light beams, lurking along the river to grab anything not cautious enough to avoid the shallows.

Jacie ruled out the river.

The streams that fed into the river were a far safer source of water.

A day later of exploring upstream, they found the perfect spot, where a stream widened into a pool about twenty feet across, and was at most two feet deep, with a clearly visible sandy bottom, peppered with a few rocks at the edges. Rainbow scaled fish flitted in and out of the rock-cast shadows. Poison dart frogs, neon green spots glowing against inky black, hopped along the broad leaves of plants overhanging the pool. A basilisk zipped across, feet barely rippling the surface.

Over the past week, they'd hiked in mid afternoon and stayed til midnight or 1 a.m., perched up in the fig tree, its broad branches as comfortable as a chair. Multiple species, from mama Baird's tapirs with watermelon striped babies, to slender *Leptocyon* dogs like Chihuahua-sized foxes, to slim-necked ornithaurs, clawed toes softly tapping along the jungle floor detritus, sipped from the stream.

But no kaleidoscope jaguars.

Jacie identified multiple piles of dried-up jaguar scat. She measured broad, webbed paw prints in the damp mud by the stream. She'd seen scrapes on tree trunks from thick sharp claws, marking out territory.

Once she caught a whiff of a honeysuckle and musk. Anna, the matriarch of the nearby village of Orinajos de los Rios, had told her if she smelled honeysuckle, the jaguars were near.

*Probably watching her and Dani.*

Anna, a plump woman whose fierce black eyes belied her silver-streaked braids and grandmotherly bosom, also told them that the jags were the smartest thing in the jungle.

Including *them*, was the unspoken comment.

The jags weren't the biggest predator out here. Quetzalcoatli, medium sized carnivorous dinosaurs native to Mexicatl, served as apex predators, preying upon anything from tapirs to jaguars to villagers. Jacie had never seen one in person, but she had a library of field guides at home from the various worlds she visited, all with color plates illustrating different species. It was a scary-looking dinosaur, all teeth and claws attached to a stocky, muscular body.

But they were rare, even rarer than the kaleidsocope jaguars, with very large ranges. Maybe an individual every square hundred miles in the jungle, more in open areas.

Regardless, Jacie suspected their presence was one of the reasons for the jaguar's abilities.

Here in the world of Mexicatl, magic was so abundant Jacie's world crossing took barely any effort on her part. Many species had evolved to use magic as well. The kaleidoscope jaguars were the prime example.

Like the jaguars of Central and South America, they had beautifully patterned coats of warm tan with black rosettes. But they possessed the ability to change color into a fractal pattern that mirrored the surrounding vegetation. It was both camouflage and a lure; Jacie had read that howler monkeys, fascinated by the shifting, sparkling colors, would creep up to examine the jaguars ... before becoming their lunch.

Jacie shifted on the branch to check her watch. 5:15 p.m. She sighed. Another forty five minutes before the sun set, then it'd get dark quickly. She slapped at a mosquito that landed on her forehead, then itched at her arm.

The whining and clicking of insects increased as the sun dipped lower. Jacie swatted at her ear and came away with blood and squashed insect parts on her fingertips.

Above her, Dani snored lightly.

5:40 p.m.

A soft floral scent tickled her nose. Honeysuckle. A jaguar? She reached up, grabbed Dani's booted foot, and tugged once. Dani awakened instantly, peering down at Jacie.

Jacie tapped her nose and pointed down to the stream, then looked back down herself.

She couldn't see anything unusual. The water surface was smooth. No ripples or scattered mirrored reflections. Certainly no two hundred plus pound cat.

Suddenly, the honeysuckle scent was all around her, so thick she could taste it. Something poked her foot, the tip of a sharp claw penetrating the leather and waxed canvas of her Army issue jungle boot.

Jacie stiffened, all muscles tight, and twisted to look behind her.

Flashes of dappled green and brown twinkled and spun, mesmerizing in the fading soft light of the setting sun.

*Hola*, it said, the throaty voice rumbling in her head.

The jaguar popped into view, one big spotted paw resting on her boot. It was otherwise crouched comfortably on the branch, pointedly between Jacie and the tree trunk. Looking off to its right at a forty-five-degree angle, it yawned, displaying two-inch canines and a rough pink tongue, all the while watching her with one narrowed chartreuse eye.

"Hi?" Jacie said back, aloud. Dani, above her, was silent. Jacie couldn't spare a glance up at her.

*Let's chat*, the jaguar said, leaping off the branch and into the stream, twenty feet below. *Leave the weapon behind.*

Three smaller scintillating blobs leapt after it—not *it*, must be a *her* —and popped in view as smaller, rangier, fluffier versions of the female jaguar once they splashed down into the stream.

Jacie gulped, finally glancing up at a white-faced Dani. "You heard her?" she asked. Dani nodded, taking off the rifle and hooking its strap around a branch.

They both climbed down to talk to the jaguar.

———

THE SUN HAD SET. Jacie and Dani sat on the muddy, leaf-covered ground near the stream. Jacie's butt was cold, mud soaking through her pants. Dani, always serene, seemed to be ignoring the mud, her attention solely on the jaguar, who lounged a few feet in front of them between them and the stream. Her cubs splashed and played in the stream, catching red-spotted, bright blue frogs that glowed in the rising moonlight. The buzzing and whining of night insects, the hoarse calls of toads, the distant deep roars of the howler monkeys: all the noises of the night melded together.

The jaguar's tail was twitching, the black and cream tip like a metronome.

*So, you traveled here, using your incredible gift, to steal me or one of my cubs,* she said. *Sell us into slavery. And why shouldn't I kill you and feed you to them?*

In the five years of shifting doorways across different worlds and catching any number of animals, Jacie had never had anything she hunted talk back to her. They were animals, incredible, awesome, amazing animals, that she made sure would be kept safe and healthy. She had rules, rules her clients had to adhere to. No trophy hunts. Top notch veterinary care. Appropriate habitat.

And now, she couldn't escape the thought: what if those animals just hadn't had the ability to communicate to her? She looked at Dani helplessly.

Dani looked as stricken as Jacie. "In our world," she said to the jaguar, "we have lost so much of the natural world, that the only way some species survive is in captivity. Others are kept as ambassadors for their species, in hopes of inspiring other humans to care for their environment."

*That may be necessary, in your world. You think that is the case* here, *in Mexicatl?* The tail tip twitched faster. *My friend Anna told me about you. They don't need me in a cage to care for the jungle. And what would my presence, in your world, do to preserve* your *world?*

"Nothing," Jacie said. "Nothing. Nothing except feed the ego of a rich, vain woman."

*What would you have me do with you?* The jaguar stood and stalked over to Jacie, her breath hot against Jacie's face, that honeysuckle sweetness rolling over Jacie. Her canines were very, very close to Jacie's face. And throat.

The night was quiet, awaiting her answer.

*Too* quiet.

A ten-foot-tall reptilian form roared and straightened by the edge of the far end of the pool, blocking the light from the rising moon, no longer any need for stealth.

A quetzalcoatl.

The cubs screeched, ran behind their mother, and blinked out, leaving an afterimage of moonlit leaves and branches. The jaguar herself stood, ears pinned back, pale green eyes wide with the whites showing, and snarled.

"The rifle," Jacie said to Dani, who nodded and snuck to the fig tree and focused on climbing, not the beast at the edge of the pool. Jacie didn't know if the sedative, enough to take down a jaguar, would do anything to the quetzal, but at least Dani would be out of immediate range.

The quetzal ignored Dani, taking short deliberate steps through the water towards the jaguar. As it got closer, Jacie could make out details: short but strong front arms, heavily muscled rear legs, and a thick, five-foot-long tail; four-fingered paws tipped with gleaming ebony eight inch claws; and a long narrow snout filled with stained, serrated teeth. It looked bigger and meaner and way scarier than the picture in the book.

Yet, for all that it was death coming for them, the quetzal was beautiful. Its iridescent scales gleamed like rainbow obsidian. Black and blue feathers formed a crest around its head, then flowed down its spine. Jacie had expected the smell of carrion, but the quetzal just smelled dry and dusty, like feathers kept in a dry attic too long.

Jacie stood and placed her hand on the jaguar's shoulder. Her coat, soft beneath Jacie's fingers, tingled like small static electrical shocks.

*Can you get my cubs away, with your gift?* the jaguar asked, her fear for her cubs a tidal wave.

"It doesn't work that way," Jacie said miserably. "I find crossing points and trigger them. I can't make something out of nothing."

The quetzal swung its head back and forth, looking at the jaguar, then Jacie, then back to the jaguar, then crouched and sprang like a striking snake, so fast Jacie couldn't think.

All she could do was shove herself in front of the jaguar, raise her hands, and, screaming, *push*.

———

JACIE WOKE with a pounding headache and parched mouth, so weak she couldn't sit up. Her left hand ached. She squinted. An IV catheter pierced her hand.

She was lying in a narrow four-poster bed built of a creamy tan wood, draped with sheer, finely woven mosquito nets. A white cotton sheet that smelled of honeysuckle had been pulled over her. It felt soft against her bare skin. Her hair was unbound and loose against the pillow.

Beyond the netting she could see whitewashed plaster walls. The room was small, maybe ten by ten feet. The walls were punctuated by deep windows, hung with breezy white curtains embroidered with bright scarlet, soft pink, and vibrant orange hibiscus flowers along the edges. Gently fluttering, they let through both morning sunlight and a soft breeze.

A rattan armchair with a green and white striped pillow was off to her left. Closer to her, between the bed and the chair, was a metal IV stand, with a bag of fluids dangling and an IV line leading from it to her hand. She wanted to yank out the catheter, but didn't even have the energy for that.

A wooden nightstand with water-stained top was to her right. A green ceramic pitcher of water and a blue-tinged glass sat atop it, just out of reach even if she had the strength. Next to the pitcher was an iridescent navy blue feather.

The scent of honeysuckles doubled, and the jaguar rose from

where she'd been laying, at the foot of the bed. *You are finally awake,* she said.

"Where am I?" Jacie asked, voice raspy. It hurt to talk.

*Anna's.* The jaguar paused. *You nearly died. Thank you for saving us.*

"The quetzal?"

*In pieces.* Many *small pieces.* The jaguar sounded distinctly satisfied. *I groomed it out of your hair while Dani sought help.*

"How long?"

*A week. Now rest. I will get Dani and Anna.* She padded out of the room, big paws silent on the stone floor.

———

DANI RUSHED IN, crying, with Anna close behind, carrying a tray with a glazed umber ceramic bowl. "I thought you'd never wake up," Dani sobbed, pushing open the netting and grabbing Jacie's right hand and squeezing.

Anna shrugged and spoke to Jacie. "I told her you would. It took two healers, but they fixed everything you broke." Her dark eyes were worried. "You'll need another week of bed rest, and a few more sessions, but you should be as back to normal as you can be."

"Can be?" Jacie repeated.

Dani picked up a strand of Jacie's hair and held it in front of Jacie's face. It gleamed a soft warm silver. Not a trace of inky black remained. Jacie's throat tightened. In the big scheme of things, it wasn't important, she was alive, Dani was alive, the cubs and the jaguar were safe, but ... her hair. Her one vanity.

"Your eyes, too. They glow silver. They're not brown anymore." Dani smiled, though another tear fell. "It's all really, really pretty. Just different. Here, let me help you sit up, Anna has some soup for you."

Between Dani and Anna, Jacie was soon sitting, multiple pillows bracing her back. Dani was poised to feed her. "I hate this," Jacie said. "Give me that damn spoon, let me try. Gods above and below."

She ate the soup. Cilantro, sour orange, and onion accentuated tender pork and creamy beans. It tasted good. Beyond good. Delicious. Worthy of a Michelin star. Not that they had those in Mexicatl.

"Was there something in the soup?" she slurred, then slumped over, asleep.

———

SHE WOKE up again in the late afternoon, the sunlight filtering through the curtains a warm gold against the white plaster walls.

The jaguar trotted up to the bed, three bundles of scintillating whitewashed plaster and stone floor following. The cubs. Jacie, relieved, sighed. They were okay.

*Go on*, the jaguar said, opening up the mosquito netting with one paw. The first cub leaped through to the foot of Jacie's bed, popping into view as he landed heavily.

For all that they were cubs, they were *not* small. This close, Jacie estimated the cub was over a hundred pounds of gangly feline, and a year old.

*Comidoret de ranas*, he squawked. *Frogeater*. He stalked up the length of the narrow bed to her, stepping on her legs, straddling her torso, pushing his sleek round head and blocky muzzle into her silvery hair, inhaling in deep whuffs.

*That's his cub name, not you*, the jaguar said to Jacie.

She reached up and rubbed behind one soft black and cream ear. "You're so handsome," she said. He made a rumbling noise; he couldn't purr, any more than the jaguars of her world could, but she assumed this was the equivalent.

*He is curious*, the jaguar said. *He is young, and foolish, and curious.*

Jacie glanced at her. The jaguar sat, shoulders hunched in displeasure, ears down, chartreuse eyes narrowed.

*He wants to go with you. Not*, she hastily added, *as a pet to that woman who hired you. But with you.* Unspoken: would he be safe? Could she trust Jacie, once gone from this world?

Jacie knew she'd never hunt and sell another creature again. "I will keep him safe," she promised. "And bring him back whenever he wants."

The kaleidoscope jaguar nodded, then padded out of the room, two cubs following, their forms dissolving into fractal bursts of gold sunlight.

# THE WRETCHED SUNLIGHT OF SHASTA

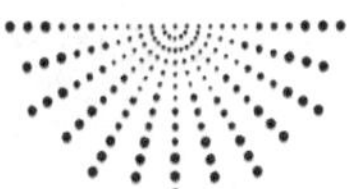

The door between worlds slammed behind Jacie with a blast of heat and blinding light, the force thrusting both her and Frogeater forward into bitter, powdery white sand.

Frogeater squawked and shook the sand from his rosette-spotted fur, his chartreuse eyes narrowed against the glare from the overhead sun.

*Where are we?* he said, his adolescent jaguar voice rumbling and squeaking in her mind.

Jacie stood, brushing sand off her shirt. The sand felt soft until she saw her fingertips were oozing fine droplets of blood.

"Careful with the sand, Frog," she said. "And I don't know. I've never been here before, and this isn't where I was aiming."

She'd been trying to get back home, to Earth. Her magic, the essence of which was finding and using the doors between worlds, had never led her literally astray before.

Frogeater, a kaleidoscope jaguar from Mexicatl, a world four doors from Earth, and newly Jacie's companion, had been anxious to visit Jacie's home, too. He, and his mother, trusted Jacie to keep him safe.

*This* place, with its vicious sand studded with cacti-like plants, wasn't home. Wasn't safe. Wasn't anything familiar.

And Jacie couldn't feel the doorway. It was like all her magic had been sucked out with the passage here.

They were stuck. Jacie had rations in her pack, but not enough for more than a day or two. And certainly not enough water, not for the two of them. Water purification tablets *and* charms, yes, if they could find water…which looked very unlikely, in the blinding expanse of powdery sand.

The air was bone dry. A faint rotten-egg smell of sulfur tickled Jacie's nose.

Frog pulled his lips up, squinted his eyes, stuck out his tongue. *Stinks.*

The sky was brilliant cloudless cerulean blue, the sun blazing white hot high overhead. She jiggled her shoulders, loosened the waistband of the pack, trying to get her backpack from sticking to her chambray shirt and her shirt from plastering against her back. Her long silver hair, bright against her tanned face, was pulled back into a braid, but she could feel sweat pooling against the roots.

It was quiet, too, not even a breeze to stir up the sand or rustle the spines of the plants.

A shadow rushed over them, and both Frog and Jacie looked up, squinting.

It was a helicopter—or, similar enough to, that's what Jacie would call it. Running silently, somehow, despite the rotating blade atop, and the smaller rotator on the long tail. Bulbous main body, made of matte black material, stark against the blue sky, with windows wrapping around the front to the side. One side solid, the other, they could see as the copter circled above them, with an open door.

Jacie could see a pilot through the front windows, but no details; then a figure, swathed in white fabric, leaned out through the open door.

"What the hell—doing out here?—a lift?" the person called. A husky feminine voice.

Jacie waved frantically, and the helicopter landed twenty yards out, the silent wind from the blades whipping strands of her hair loose from her braid.

The woman beckoned them aboard. Up close, Jacie could see she was wearing silky white robes and a head scarf loosely wound around her hair and face. Bright copper eyes framed by dark chestnut skin met Jacie's eyes.

"You're twenty miles into the Kashasta Waste, you idiots," she said. "Got a death wish?"

Jacie bristled. "Not here by choice," she said. "And I want, *we* want, to leave as soon as possible."

Frog jumped up into the copter, nodded at the white-clad woman, then curled up on the floor and began grooming his saucer-sized feet.

"Stop!" the woman barked.

Frog froze. The woman grabbed a whisk broom and brushed his paws off. "Both of you with a death wish. That stuff is poison. Where are you from, that you know nothing?"

Rock and a hard place. Or rather, death sand and sunlight.

"Not this world," Jacie admitted.

The woman narrowed her eyes. "Hmph. Buckle in." She passed some straps with hooks, mimed attaching them to her belt. The other ends of the straps were looped around a central bar.

"Can your cat tolerate a waist strap?" she asked.

*Yes.*

The woman started, obviously hearing Frog in her head, then hooked a belt around Frog's chest and attached it to more straps. "Linnie, get us home."

"Sure thing, ma," the pilot said. Linnie. The copter rose, still silent, and they sped west.

———

THE COPTER FLIGHT took about twenty minutes. The white sand extended under them for most of it, then stopped abruptly, separated from the familiar (at least to Jacie, who lived on a small parcel of land in Topanga Canyon, if not Frog, who was born in thick tropical jungle) sages and prickly pear of coastal chaparral by a deep stony ditch, at least twenty feet across. In the distance, before they landed, Jacie could see a sliver of blue. An ocean?

The copter landed about a quarter mile from the ditch, just within a chain-link fenced area, about one square mile, that included neat rows of large tents, big enough to house at least ten people per; three more copters; and several large areas covered by canopies, shading tables and benches. In the farthest corner she had seen orchards, fruit trees with stunted branches, as they landed. Beyond the far fence were gently rolling hills and dunes.

A handful of people, all dressed like the woman who'd found them, in white robes, hustled about, carrying boxes or baskets.

The camp smelled like sage and burnt human waste, overlaid with a tang of ocean brine.

Frog sneezed.

"Names?" the woman asked as Jacie unbuckled herself, then Frog.

"Jacie and Frog. Frogeater."

"Hmph. No frogs, anymore." She held out her hand, thin with gnarled knuckles. "Hope you can eat fish and grubs. I'm Guerita. Inheritomancer, Warleader, and now Shepherd to those who remain. Linnie, my daughter, is one of our pilots."

Linnie turned to look at them, smiled. She was young, in her twenties, Jacie guessed, and wore the ubiquitous white gown, though lacked the head scarf. Her hair billowed around her dark face in rich black curls. Her golden eyes were bright with curiosity above high cheekbones.

"Can I pet him?" she asked.

"He's his own person," Jacie said. "Ask him."

"May I?"

Frog stepped forward, butted his head against her hand, and rumbled softly. *Ears.* He nudged her hand til Linnie stroked his ears, her eyes wide.

Guerita shrugged back her head scarf, exposing a narrow face, lined with age. Linnie got those gorgeous cheekbones from her mother, as well as the metallic eyes. But Guerita's hair was cropped to tight grey curls against her skull.

"Welcome to Shasta. What's left of the world." Her mouth twisted, and she gestured them forward.

————

GUERITA WHISKED Frog's fur and Jacie's clothes with the broom, clearing any remaining sand. "Come on, then. Let's get you some water and cebiche."

They walked towards one of the smaller canopied areas.

"What happened here?" asked Jacie. Frog nudged her. Well, she never had been tactful. Why start now?

"You're truly from another world?" Guerita asked. Jacie nodded. "You travel by magic or science?"

"I call it magic," Jacie said. "It's a form of energy I can access, I suppose. Some worlds I've visited have so much every living creature uses it, like Frog's world of Mexicatl. Beauty and terror, all in balance." She thought of the quetzal, that feather fringed dinosaur who'd nearly made a meal of her and Frog. Of the ability of the kaleidoscope jaguars, splintering light to camouflage themselves.

"My home world doesn't have much left. Enough for me to travel, little more."

"We used to have a lot of magic," Guerita said. "My granny told me, and her ma, before she passed. Even when I was a child, you could still reach out and wield the sunlight, barehanded, for a pretty show. Light up the butterflies. But we couldn't use it for much more than our engines by then. Nothing for healing, for food production, nothing. The copters use it now. The digger blew itself out, excavating the ditch. So far the ditch is keeping the sand back, but...it blows in. Gets into everything. Our clothes, our food, our lungs.

"One hundred forty nine of us left. Some fish in the sea. More than enough, finally, to feed us, given how few of us there are now."

"But what happened?" Jacie said.

Guerita shrugged. "Human nature. Greed. Overconsumption. War, then, over limited resources. Ruin followed, and the poisoning of the land as people yanked the power out of it. I've tried reaching out, to find other communities, but the radios quit working two months ago, and there's nothing in range of our copters. There's nothing left for us. We have DNA banked, but we're a dead species still breathing.

"This is the mess tent," she said, motioning them under the khaki canvas canopy and towards a rickety aluminum table flanked by benches made of overturned buckets and planks of weather-beaten wood. "Sit. I'll get some water and food for you. After that, I have work to do in the lab, but when I can, in the next day or so, I'll talk to you about how you can perhaps help us. Check with Linnie about mess times and a cot."

In the next day or so? Jacie wanted to get out of this desolate place, *now*. But she just nodded. "Thank you."

Frog butted his broad round head against Jacie's thigh. *I don't like it here.*

"Me neither," Jacie said. She *reached*, seeking with her gut, for any sense of a door. Anything. Even on Earth, even stretching her powers, she could usually feel multiple doors, within a range of fifty miles or so. Los Angeles had half a dozen, from one at the edge of Redondo Beach Pier all the way to one near the arts and crafts utopia of the Gamble House in Pasadena. And she hadn't bought her house in Topanga for the boho lifestyle. A door to icy Kanata opened from her herb garden.

Here? Nothing. Not even a sense of the door through which they'd been thrust.

That door from Mexicatl eventually led to the state park of Bentsen-Rio Grande, on the southernmost border of Texas. Not to this world of Shasta, which *felt* so far away from Earth Jacie couldn't figure out how many worlds away it actually was.

"I can't sense anything," she whispered to Frog. "Maybe, because I was so hurt...I thought I was fully healed, but...." Battling the quetzal had nearly killed her. She was foolhardy to think she could travel already!

*You* are *strong*, insisted Frog. His green eyes, so earnest, were focused on Jacie. *I trust you. You will get your magic back, with food and rest.*

But did they have time? This world, Shasta, was dying. And it might just take them with it.

———

THE NEXT MORNING, Jacie *reached* again. And to her relief, found, to the west, towards the ocean, a glimmer, a hint, a shimmer of a memory of a door.

*Told you,* Frog said. *Wait til tomorrow. I bet we can use it then.*

Linnie met them briefly at breakfast. "Feel free to explore the camp," she told them. "Gotta run, sorry. Copter maintenance. The sand gunks up the motor."

People seemed friendly—a quick smile in their direction, a nod hello—but no one had any time to speak with them. The youngest, lanky teens, glanced shyly then away.

"Explore it is," Jacie said to Frog, after one last attempt to chat with an older man, Guerita's age. He smiled briefly, murmured, "Off to work," and disappeared between the tents.

Jacie and Frog walked along the narrow path, cleared of spiny bushes, along the fence line. Large boxy crustaceans, all purple spines and iridescent lilac carapaces, scuttled on ten legs along the outside of the chain linked fence. No birds. No mammals. Not even reptiles.

The orchard, at the far end of the camp, was citrus, limes and lemons. Dry brown leaves hung off the tips of the branches. White sand, blown by errant breezes, pillowed up against the trunks. Shriveled fruit dotted the ground and sand.

They found the pits where the latrine refuse was being burned. Frog poked at a dung beetle trundling towards the pit, jumping back as it tucked and rolled.

Dung beetles and crabs. Fish in the ocean, at least, but everything else was gone.

They passed one tent, far from the main camp, with guards at the one opening. The lab that Guerita had spoken of? Likely. But guards? Why would it be guarded?

*Chemicals*, Frog said, opening his mouth to taste and smell. *Like the sand.*

Sulfur. Jacie's nose wasn't as strong as Frog's, but the rotten stench seeped to the back of her throat.

And...

...magic?

Just a trickle, from the overhead sun to the tent. She rubbed at her arms, suddenly chilled, despite the heat. It was wrong. Jacie had never thought magic, in and of itself, could be wrong. But this was. It stank of rot and theft.

And it reached for her.

"Let's get out of here," Jacie said.

———

LUNCH WAS QUIET. And people no longer seemed quite as friendly. No one spoke to them, just ate and left.

"The door—" Jacie said, once she and Frog were alone. "I can feel it, stronger."

*Let's go. Even if you can't bring us through, we can check it out.*

A young man, wearing the ubiquitous white robes and head scarf of all the other camp personnel, lounged against the front gate, pointing a pistol-like weapon and zapping the scuttling crustaceans with bolts of light. He straightened as they approached, hanging his blaster off a loop on his belt.

"Hey there. Where's the beach?" Jacie asked. Had she noticed guards, anywhere, when they landed?

"You know nothing of the dangers of this world," the young man said.

"Um, not an answer. I just want to go see the ocean," she said.

"I'm sorry, but there is no one to escort you. Please return to the main camp."

Frog grunted and stalked towards him.

"Please return to the main camp, both you and your creature," the guard said, voice steady, despite his white knuckled grip on his blaster.

Grumbling, Jacie acquiesced. "Come on, Frog."

*We need to get out*, Frog said as they walked away.

"Tomorrow. Or even tonight," Jacie promised.

———

AFTER DINNER, Guerita found them in the sleeping tents, near the cot assigned to Jacie.

Go to bed early, Jacie had thought. Get up in the middle of the night. Find a way out.

But not now.

"You said your talent is travel," Guerita said. "There is nothing for you here, so I know you will leave, when you are able. But I have to ask: can you take us with you?"

"I don't know," Jacie said. "My powers...I was drained by travelling here. I can only hope they'll return."

"I hope so, too," Guerita said. She stared at Jacie, mouth pursed, then shook her head slowly. "I really do."

*You lied to her*, Frog said, after Guerita left.

"Not completely. I *was* drained. Now I'm better." Jacie laid back on her cot and pulled the light silk blanket over her. The air chilled quickly once the sun set, regardless of the blistering daytime heat. Her camo pants were stiff with dried sweat, as was her black tank and chambray shirt, but she wore them to sleep in anyways. "I don't trust her."

She *reached*. The door to the west beckoned. She couldn't sense what lay beyond it, but she desperately wanted to get away from Shasta.

*Don't even* think *things couldn't be worse*, warned Frog.

"I'm not about to," she said. "But I'm willing to risk it, if you are. I don't think we could get back to the gate in the wasteland, and I don't even know if it truly would go to Mexicatl. Something went wrong. Something brought us here, twisting the door."

*There's nothing here but death*, said Frog. He coughed. The sand was everywhere. *I'm willing to risk it too.*

"Tomorrow night, then."

Frog licked her hand, his tongue rasping. *Tomorrow night.*

———

THE SECOND DAY was more of the same: citrus-scented tea with briny vegetables for breakfast, and with cebiche for lunch and dinner. The fish was fresh; Jacie had seen two women leave through the gate before dawn, and returning with a netload of fish later that morning.

She was too slow to ask to join them at the gate on their way out.

"I can still see them," Jacie said to the guard, hacking in the dry air after sprinting to the gate, her hands on her knees as she caught her breath. And she could. The white of the silk robes gleamed in the first rays of dawn, not two hundred yards away, nearing the pass in the dunes that must lead to the ocean.

And the door.

"I'm sorry, but the ocean isn't safe for strangers," the guard, this time a young woman, said, hand on the grip of her holstered blaster. Twitchier than the last.

"Gotcha," Jacie said, raising her hands, backing away. Good thing Frog still dozed in the tent.

Like the afternoon before, no one wanted to talk to her.

Or was allowed to.

At lunch, she grabbed her tray (as well as a bowlful of raw fish for Frog) and surveyed the mess tent. There. Linnie.

"Hi there," Jacie said, dusting off then plopping on the bench opposite the young pilot. "What's up?"

Linnie glanced around. Leaned forward. "I can't talk to you, anymore," she said.

"You just did."

"My ma—I can't. I'm sorry."

"Dude, you are making me seriously worried about your intentions." Jacie waved her hand. "You, meaning all of you, not just you personally."

Linnie stared down at her plate. "You seem nice. And Frog—he's beautiful." She looked up quickly, then back down. "I don't want anything bad to happen to you."

"Why would something bad happen, Linnie?" Besides being stuck in this god-awful dying place.

"My ma thinks you can get us somewhere safe," she whispered. "And she has a plan to use the sun magic to strip away your magic. She got you here, she said, with her magic. So she thinks she can steal yours, to get us away. The past two days she hasn't left the lab."

Jacie thought about the blast of heat, the searing light, that yanked her and Frog into Shasta. The rotten power reaching for her from the tent.

And she thought that a mother would do anything to save her people. Her child.

"My power is gone," Jacie lied.

"Doesn't matter," Linnie said. "You know why this world is ruined? Because we sucked everything away, down to the life force. If there's something in your DNA that gave you your powers, she'll find it and steal it. It's what they did. What she did. Inheritomancy, powered by the sun."

"Help us get away, then," Jacie said. "You can fly us out of here, right?"

"I—we're all going to die, Jacie."

"Even if I was fully powered, I couldn't take all of you with me. I'll be lucky to manage me and Frog. Maybe, just maybe, a few others." She could feel the door, *calling* to her. It wanted to serve her as much as she wanted to use it. "If I promise to try, will you let us go?"

Linnie stared at her, eyes wide, frightened.

Frog sidled over to her, rubbed his face against her thigh. *Whatever you decide.*

"Meet me after dinner by the copter," Linnie said. "I'll bring the youngest. None of this is their fault. If you can get them out, please—"

"I'll try," Janie said. "That's all I can do."

———

FROG DIDN'T MIND FISH, but he was antsy with waiting, and had decided to take it out on his meal. *Dull,* he said as he wolfed down his bowlful of plain white fish at dinner. *Rather catch them myself.*

"We'll go to the beach when we get home," Jacie promised. She didn't know a good spot to fish near Malibu. She'd have to research it, once they got home. She picked at her dinner. She didn't think she'd go out for sushi for a month. "Here, you can finish mine." She sat her plate down on the ground.

Frog crinkled his nose. *Onions,* he said, batting the plate away.

"Picky," Linnie said from behind them. She lowered her voice. "I put robes in your backpack. Change into them. I don't know what to do about Frog."

"We'll figure it out," Jacie said. "Come on, Frog. Let's get some rest."

They walked back to their sleeping tent as the sun set, streaks of scarlet and coral painting the sky.

"Some of this world is pretty," Jacie said. Frog grunted.

She dug through her pack. The white silk robe was folded neatly at the bottom. Jacie pulled it over her head, sashing the waist as she'd seen others wear it. The head scarf, though, was hopeless. It kept slipping off. She didn't see any pins.

"Can you hide?" she asked Frog. "Do your kaleidoscope thing?"

*I think so,* he said. *There is so little magic here.* His form splintered into reflections of the sunset, then dulled, reflecting the black of the shadows in the tent. *Can you see me?*

"Nope," Jacie said. He was shafts of dull shadow, nothing more. "Let's go." They slipped out of the tent, Jacie gripping the head scarf around her shoulders like a shawl, Frog flickering to match the twilight-darkened stains on the khaki canvas tent.

They reached the copter, if not *unseen,* on Jacie's part, at least unnoticed.

Linnie sat at the controls, flipping switches, muttering under her breath. A half dozen teenagers had strapped themselves into the body of the copter. Their eyes, copper and gold and bronze, shimmered in the light of the rising moon. Frog joined them, letting Jacie strap him in.

"You *do* have some of your power, right?" Linnie asked, not pausing.

"Yes," Jacie said, sliding into the seat next to Linnie. "But I don't know if it's enough for seven of you—"

"Six." Linnie activated the rotors. Jacie couldn't help but expect the *whup whup whup* of a regular helicopter, but the copter rose silently.

—then *screeched*, the sound of metal being yanked and forced to obey, and stopped, just ten feet off the ground.

In front of them was Guerita, hands raised. Light emanated from her palms, wrapped around the copter. Held it.

"Ma—"

"Let us go!" Jacie yelled. "I'm taking your children to safety!"

"One hundred forty two more!" Guerita bellowed back. "I don't care if I have to rip you and your cat to protein particles, I'm getting *everyone* out!"

"MA!" Linnie had one hand on the controls, the other stretched towards her mother. Beseeching.

The copter shrieked like it was alive, the blades of the rotors like the wings of a struggling bird.

"I don't have enough power on my own," Linnie whispered to Jacie. "That's why I'm just a pilot, not working with my ma in the lab."

Jacie gripped Linnie's hand, holding the controls. Reached her other hand back to Frog, buried her fingers into his plush neck fur.

"You have us," Jacie said. "Use us."

"I—okay." *Something* pulled at Jacie, pulled through her to Frog, then snapped back to Linnie.

Light burst out from Linnie's hand, knocking Guerita to the ground.

Her silk robes ignited, burning fierce blue in the haze of twilight, sending acrid puffs of sand-scented smoke into the sky.

Linnie sobbed as the copter lurched back into her control. She didn't wait to see what happened to her mother. She flew them towards the ocean.

———

THE OCEAN STRETCHED BEFORE THEM, the last magenta of sunset reflecting lilac off the cresting waves. The fresh salty tang overcame the bitterness of the white sand.

"There," Jacie said, pointing to a small rocky cove. "The door is there." She could see it, shimmering in the frothy surf.

Linnie landed the copter. "Take care of them," she said.

"Come with us," Jacie said. "With your help, I can bring all of you, I know it."

"I'll help, but I can't go with you," Linnie said. "How do you think I knew how to take and use power? I don't deserve to go."

"Everyone deserves a second chance."

"I have to see what happened to Ma. It's okay, Jacie." Linnie squeezed her hands. "You go. Maybe, if you can come back, some day. But not now."

Jacie thought of the dying citrus. The encroaching poisonous sand. The searing sunlight. The camp wouldn't last more than another season, if that long.

"Okay," she lied.

Linnie leaned forward, gold eyes dimmed, and kissed her on the forehead. "Thank you. Now go."

———

JACIE STOOD in front of the door, knee deep in warm ocean water, camo pants sodden against her legs. *Something* bumped against her shin, and she gulped down a shriek. The ocean, at least, might survive, even if the humans didn't.

"Everyone ready?" she asked, not waiting for the soft murmurs of assent, then stepped forward, Frog pressed against her side, tail twined around her wrist, and the children behind them.

The door opened eagerly, so much that Jacie wondered if the doors had any sentience of their own. If it wanted to help.

She stepped through, then Frog, then the children.

The door flared, then closed, as the last child sloshed through.

—into a new world, with a sky of pale blue and a field of tall, gently waving grasses. A flock of green and black birds flew overhead, their raucous squawks competing with the whir and chirrups of insects. The smell of rich loamy earth, life-filled earth, overwhelmed them.

—into a new home.

# CRATE TRAINING

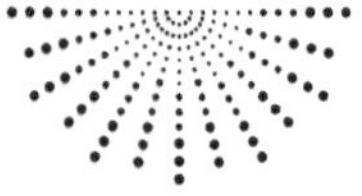

"But I don't wanna go to the kennel," whined Jeffie.

"It's a blood moon, my darling," I said, crouching down to ruffle his fluffy blond hair. Eight years old, and already willing to challenge his Alpha momma! "Remember what happened last time, when you didn't?"

"I ate Mrs Crosby's Siamese cat," he muttered. "And Mr Peterson's Shih Tzu."

"And?"

"And I chased the Booker twins, and almost bit them." His eyes, already wolfish, flashed green at me. "They were mean to me at school. They deserved it."

"I'm sure they did, but what does a leader do?" I asked, taking his hand. I opened the heavy oak door to the concrete-floored basement, inhaling the rich musky scent of the other cubs, already settled into their iron-barred crates, savagely attacking their chew toys and bully sticks.

Jeffie sighed. "A leader leads, with mercy and justice. They don't administer capri —capricious punishment."

He shifted effortlessly into a rangy, cream colored wolf cub, all gangly limbs and the tiniest bit of an underbite. He rolled his green eyes at me then trotted into his crate.

"Good puppy!" I said. I tossed in a special treat, a whole rabbit purchased from the neighbor two doors down. They bred the rabbits for food. It was convenient.

"If they're still mean next month," I whispered, shutting and locking the crate door, "I'll let you bite them as hard as you want."

No one said the alpha mom couldn't be a vindictive bitch.

# THE BODY MAGE'S FOOT

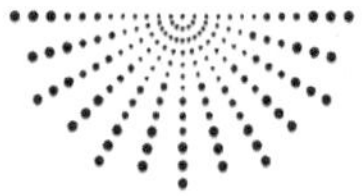

Thirty miles away, buried in the soft white sand, the severed end of Christa's left ankle ached, a muted pulsation of longing.

Her foot *missed* her.

A broken body mage soldier. Broken until she had all of herself back together.

Christa opened her eyes. She was in a hospital room, by herself, white painted walls, white ceiling, white floors, from what little she could see of the floor. Softly beeping machines matched her breathing and heart rate. A catheter firmly snugged into the vein on the back of her right hand dripped room temperature fluids into her. Her skin, normally a golden tan, looked pallid against the white sheets. The big, uncurtained windows, two on either wall (*corner room*, she catalogued, ever the soldier), were open, letting in the sweet odor of plumeria. It didn't overcome the reek of bleach, but it helped.

Morning, based on the light and her internal compass. Still on the resort island of Saint Malloria, based on the temperature and that same bright sunlight.

A baby blue cotton hospital blanket pressed down up the stump of her lower leg.

*A small screaming figure, wielding a freakin' sword, bearing down on her as she scrambled to unjam her rifle. Grenades lobbed at her, at their position behind some of the big rocks that dotted the sandy beach, grenades that J.D. and Tommy and Ruth tossed back, like a mad game of catch. Gunpowder and blood permeated the air with copper and saltpeter.*

*This was a corporate/union dispute they were hired to put down, on this island??? More like an all-out battle.*

*The berserking manager, hopped up on who knew what, reached her, just as Christa raised her piece of shit lowest-cost rifle like a baseball bat. If the resort union had bothered to arm her squad properly, as contracted, her squad would've already prevailed against the management.*

*The man sliced down as Christa, shrieking, knocked his head to kingdom come, augmenting her strike with all the powers she could focus, pulling strength from the bloody, sandy earth.*

*She couldn't help it, she did it, she yanked strength out of the earth.*

*Christa lurched to one side, the world off balance, and fell, as the aerial bombs landed, and everything went black and red.*

The berserking manager had cut her foot off.

And it looked like even though *she* was in a union hospital, her foot wasn't.

The door snicked open.

"Good morning!" A young man, filling out his mint green scrubs nicely, stepped into the room, his tanned face smooth with that plastic look of friendly concern. "I'm Nurse Joe. How are you feeling this morning?"

"Like I'm not all here," Christa said.

"Ah, you're joking! That is good. Humor helps with recovery."

"I don't think it's going to grow my foot back."

"Ah, yes, your foot."

"Why is my foot not attached?" She could *feel* it. To the west. Their last position—

*—bombs, J.D. screaming, everything black and red, so red—*

"It's in our contracts. Everything needs to be collected. We can heal, we just need all the pieces—"

*—so red—*

Nurse Joe stuck a thermometer in her mouth, shutting her up.

"Your friends are dead, Mage Christa. I'm sorry. Multiple bombs. They couldn't identify what belonged to who. It was all buried."

Pieces? Buried, all together?

Christa shoved away his hand even as the thermometer beeped.

"Did you idiots not read the contracts? We are"—*were*— "a squad of *body mages*. In a situation like *that* everything, everyone, is supposed to be burned."

Her foot was *afraid*.

But not as afraid as everyone else on this island should be.

Greedy managers and CEOs? The union was going to have a hell of a lot more to worry about, and soon.

Tommy. Ruth. J.D. If they were dead—her heart ached, just *ached*, her friends, her squadmates, her family!—then what was going to happen next was not just the union's fault.

She thought about her last strike. Dragging power out of the bloody sand. Priming it.

It would be her fault.

———

CHRISTA HOBBLED to the jeep on crutches. They'd cut off her khaki uniform when she got to the hospital, they said, so she borrowed a pair of the ubiquitous mint green scrubs. The scrubs hung off her small bony frame. She'd used too much energy. It would take time to replace her muscles, time and rest and food and meditation.

Nurse Joe passed her on to the head of the hospital, Commander Franks, a sturdy, dark haired woman in her forties, just a few years older than Christa. She towered over Christa a good six inches.

Body mages didn't have to be big to be good soldiers. Just good body mages. And Christa was one of the best. Had to be, to survive this long.

"A squad of flamethrowers will meet us at the site," Franks said quietly.

"Militia?" At Franks' nod, she asked, "Do they know what they might face?"

"They've been briefed."

Christa didn't know what she was going to do about her foot. It pulsed at her. Weaker. She still hoped she could recover it. Hoped that nothing else was moving under the sand.

Hoped that the flamethrowers *had* been adequately briefed.

Nurse Joe had fed her, at least, real food, not hospital crap, while she waited for Franks to get things organized. A whole roasted chicken. She'd devoured it in sixty seconds flats, breaking the little bones and sucking on them when she'd stripped each bone of any last bit of flesh.

That display of ravening hunger fueled their concern, more than her warnings.

They never truly *believed*, the people who hired body mages. Just thought about the augmented strength and healing that meant they could hire a mere squad, not a whole company, to settle any issues that required physical force.

Never believed. Not until the bad things happened.

Dead body mages, pieces of dead body mages, were always, *always* to be burned.

Because flesh wanted to live. Body mage or not, flesh wanted to live, but with the magic a body mage channeled, that flesh might live after death.

And every living thing needed to eat.

———

THE COVE *LOOKED* PEACEFUL. Turquoise waves lapped at the soft tan sand. The flamethrower squad sat in the sparse shade of the tall coconut trees, chatting amongst themselves, eyeing her dismissively as she hopped out of the jeep, crutches digging deep in the soft sand.

No hint of blood or death.

Not on top of the sand, anyways.

"How many days ago?" Christa asked.

"Three," Franks said. "You were out for three days. Honestly, we didn't even think you were going to make it."

Christa wondered if they would've burned her body at the hospital, if she'd died there. Or put her into a cabinet drawer in the morgue, to beat her way out.

Three days. Small pieces, ears, fingers, noses, wiggled immediately, and the power usually petered out after twelve hours or so. Larger pieces, say four to six inches, a hand, a scalp, a lobe of liver, would start a little later, last a little longer. But if the pieces were intact? or worse, if they coalesced, into a pile of hungry meat? It could take two or three days for them to rise.

Her missing foot pulsed. Christa hopped across the beach like a human flesh detector, til she circled into a closing spiral over a hump in the sand.

She couldn't feel other bits, not close to her foot.

It was trying to get away. It was scared. Scared of the other pieces. It knew she was still alive, it wanted to be a part of her, and it had burrowed away from its burial place, as far and as fast as it could. Now that she'd found her foot, she could trace the faint line in the sand, the path of her foot, that led to a mound near the flamethrower squad.

"Come to mama," Christa whispered, dropping to her knees. She dug, windmilling her arms and spraying sand everywhere, til she dug a hole three feet deep, til she could see the flash of sparkling champagne polish painted on her toenails through the ripped-up leather of her boots.

The toes wiggled at her.

She grabbed her foot and yanked it out of the hole. They'd buried it boot-on, but the cut edge still seemed fresh. The visible toes were a healthy pink.

The magic of a body mage.

She could feel the sutured skin on her stump splitting, blood slicking the bandages, opening up the wound on her leg, so she could stick her foot back on.

She pulled up the scrubs bottom on her left leg and started ripping off the bandages on her stump.

"MAGE!"

Commander Franks, her eyes wide, her mouth agape, waving wildly in the direction of the flamethrower squad.

Christa looked.

The mound *wasn't*.

Instead of a mound of sand, burying her squadmates, a misshapen *thing* uncovered itself. She saw J.D.'s face peering out from under an arm extending from an abdomen. That flat belly, that six pack, that was Ruth, at least the lower part of the torso. The twitching pecs on top were all Tommy. Ruth's head was stuck between the shoulder blades, and Tommy's at the small of the back. Legs and arms, fingers and toes, sprouted from the edges of the misshapen torso, until it formed a fleshy Catherine wheel, with gnashing teeth.

From the size, Christa could tell the thing had just absorbed any scraps, just adding to the mass.

It glistened in the late morning sunlight, streaked with gelling fluids as everything meshed and flexed. It didn't stink. It smelled, yes, of rich bloody meat, but it didn't reek of decay or piss or shit.

The flamethrower squad did. Even from ten yards away Christa could smell they'd all shit themselves.

She didn't have time to put her foot on. She pushed herself up, hopping on her right foot, and tucked the left under her arm.

This wasn't going to go well.

"Light up the meatball, you idiots!" she bellowed. "Flame it!"

The meatball twitched at her voice, then scrabbled to the closest flamethrower, pulling itself along the sand with a flurry of limbs. Meatballs weren't sentient. Just hungry. It grabbed the soldier with multiple arms and pulled him close. Close enough to feed.

The screams started.

"FLAME IT!" Gods, did she have to do *everything*? She hopped past Commander Franks, towards the remaining flamethrowers.

Who *still* hadn't lit up their flames.

Once the first soldier was dead, the meatball could just absorb his mass directly.

No one, no one ever read the medium print, let alone the small. The briefings were never complete. No one ever, ever learned.

Times like this Christa wished she could just let the meatball eat. Eat and grow. They were on an island. The island could be bombed, after the meatball had run amuck. Maybe, maybe, if the big bad happened once, if a meatball ran wild, the little problems, like now, wouldn't have to occur nearly every. Freakin'. Time.

Nah. People never learned.

She didn't want to put her foot down, and she couldn't operate a flamethrower one handed, even if she could yank one from one of the squad members.

The meatball had consumed two more flamethrowers. Only three remaining. Man, this one was fast.

Christa sighed, then steadied herself against the trunk of a coconut tree.

Two flamethrowers left.

She drew up power from the sand, from the earth, through her right foot. Her left foot twitched against her armpit and trembled in anticipation.

One flamethrower left, frozen in fear.

Christa pulled up more power. Her nerves zinged and her blond hair crackled in a nimbus of electricity.

No more flamethrowers. Just her and the meatball. J.D., Ruth, Tommy. Christa stretched out her hand, stroked one of the arms.

"I'm sorry, guys," she said. And *pulled*, pulled power from the meatball, linking it to the earth power, until the hungrier earth drained the meatball to a wispy husk of sinew and bone.

"Burn it this time, okay?" Christa said as she hopped past Franks, back to the jeep.

She put her foot on the back seat, then pulled herself up next to it. Unwrapped her bandage. Snugged the raw edge of her foot against the moist edge of her stump.

Leaned back, closed her eyes, and let her flesh coalesce to Franks' howls as she burnt the dregs of the meatball.

*J.D. Ruth. Tommy.*

# THE GIRL WHO CREATED A MECHANICO MENAGERIE

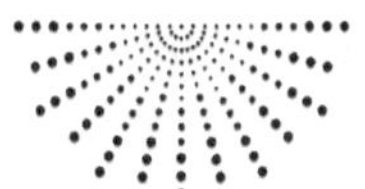

The mechanico crow dive bombed Professor James Askish with an earsplitting quork of joy.

Then yanked out a tuft of Askish' cotton-candy pink hair.

Jackheart, the crow, adored bright colors. His own metallic wings gleamed a sedate indigo in the yellow gaslight of the Magicks and Engineering lecture hall.

*You could hear a pinion drop*, thought Jacqueline, given the stunned silence of the attendees of Askish' lecture on *Dynamics of Interstitial Magicks Upon Water and Earth Workings*.

And indeed one stylized feather did fall, batted loose by Askish, the shaft piercing the scuffed oak floors of the lecture hall with a solid thunk.

"Jackheart!" Jacqueline called, and the crow, with a last derisive caw, flew to her shoulder and perched there, his steel claws piercing her woolen jacket and linen blouse.

And her flesh.

"Loosen up," she hissed. The crow shifted, the tiny joints in each leg and toe clacking. He smelled of hot steel and grease and blood.

"Student West." Professor Askish dabbed at a spot of blood welling up on his age-lined hand. His blue-eyed glare made her stomach clench.

"Report to the Dean of Discipline immediately."

Jackheart offered her the strands of soft pink hair with a soft quork.

———

THE DEAN'S office was on the ground floor of Jericho Hall, the University's main building, a centuries-old Gothic inspired gray stoned building with renowned stained glass windows. It was a quick walk across the grassy quad with its herb gardens (culinary, medicinal, and magickal) from Engineering's Smithson Hall.

Smithson Hall, a more recent addition constructed of red brick, was completely piped for gas lighting and heat, and boasted modern plumbing to boot. Jacqueline had heard rumors that it would be wired for electricity if it was deemed not too risky.

She probably wouldn't be here for any renovations.

This wasn't the first time she'd had to report to the Dean of Discipline.

Not the first time one of her mechanico menagerie had misbehaved.

And she feared it would be the last. At least, the last time at University.

She plucked a stem of lavender from the nearest herb bed, sniffed it, and tucked it behind her ear.

Jackheart flexed his toes and tilted forward.

"Don't you dare," Jacqueline muttered.

Catanape was—should be—curled up on her leather bed in the sun, on the broad window seat in Jacqueline's bedroom slash office slash workroom in Crawley Tower, basking like any real cat. Nose-bloom, the spaniel, would likely be inching closer and closer to Catanape, wanting to cuddle and warm his joints too.

Sharpears, the owl project-in-progress, had a perch in the window as well, though she wasn't quite complete. Jacqueline had about a weeks' worth of tinkering to finish her, tweaking the power source to accept moonlight as well as sunlight through her great orange eyes.

Jacqueline entered Jericho Hall and turned down the hallway to the right, her rubber-soled shoes squeaking against the waxed cherry floorboards. Magelights bound in amber glass bulbs perfumed the hallway with attar of roses, sweet against the beeswax of the cherry floors. Portraits of the former Deans lined either wood-paneled wall, in artistic styles from overly realistic to broad nebulous strokes.

University gossip had it that the portraits were imbued with an echo of their subject's personality.

If so, they were all judging her as she walked by.

Unfit. Scattered. Dangerous.

Jacqueline allowed the latter. *Dangerous.* That had a nice ring to it.

But she was just as bright as any other student. Just as fit, just as deserving. And Jacqueline could do more with mechanicos than any other student or master: her work required intense focus.

It was just that was all she wanted to do, create fantastical creatures of steel and joints and magic. And if any other course of study had no discernible application to her creations, then it was a waste of her time.

The Dean of Discipline's office was at the end of the hallway, past that of the Dean of Magical Arts, the Dean of Engineering, and the Dean of Students. And all the other Deans she'd never met.

Never annoyed.

She knocked on the heavy oak door.

"Come in, Student West."

The Dean of Discipline was a slight woman, hair silvered at her temples, with a voice to seduce angels and a wit to skewer demons.

Rumor had it the Dean had done both.

Or maybe vice-versa.

"That is the creature that attacked Professor Askish? *Visiting* Professor Askish, from the top University in this country?" the Dean asked, leaning back into her leather chair. The Dean sat, not behind her ornately carved burled desk, but next to it, legs tucked up like a schoolgirl. She wore a simple green woolen gown, with a watermelon tourmaline focus crystal pendant on a silver chain around her slender neck.

Jackheart cocked his head, gears clinking. *Shiny.* Jacqueline knew how her crow thought.

"Well, Jackheart really didn't mean any harm, it's just he loves bright colors—"

The Dean narrowed her flinty gray eyes.

"Yes, ma'am." *How did the Dean find out so quickly?*

"I know everything that happens on this campus, Student West."

Jackheart quivered. *Shiny!*

"If that creature flies at me, it is you who will dismantle it, Student West, and melt its power source."

Jacqueline grabbed the mechanico crow around his body and tucked him under her arm. "I'm very sorry, ma'am, it won't happen again—"

"Yet it nearly just did." The Dean tapped her chin thoughtfully. "Let me see if I recall correctly. The cat mechanico ruined the Benefactor's Supper last fall, did it not, chasing an enchanted mouse around the kitchen? Donations to the University are down ten percent since."

"The enchanted mouse wasn't my fault," protested Jacqueline. "And if it wasn't for it being enchanted, and Catanape being hungry for magic, Catanape would never have—"

"And the dog. The dog is the reason the stable burned down this winter, correct? Chasing more vermin, without the common sense the gods above granted to flesh and blood animals, to avoid the gas lines. Luckily it was over the Winter Holiday, and the grooms woke up in time to rescue the few horses in residence. Regardless, replacing the stables cost more than a year of your tuition.

"You are costing this University money, Student West."

"If my research bears out, ma'am, the financial windfall—"

"*If.* If you didn't destroy the entire campus in the meantime. I'm very sorry, Miss West, but you are hereby expelled. We simply cannot afford you. Please remove yourself, your creatures, and your belongings by the end of the weekend."

"Dean, please—"

The Dean's sharp features softened. "You are an enterprising young woman, with immense talent. Keep your head about you, and you will find a place for your work. And be cautious: a woman traveling alone is always at risk. Avoid large spaces in the evenings; stick to small, places you can defend. A mule and a cart from the stables will be requisitioned for your belongings."

"Ma'am—"

"Shut the door behind you, Miss West."

———

IT TOOK ALL of the three days the Dean had given Jacqueline to get everything packed and ready. Raw materials, steel and gems and copper wires and ball bearings. Hammers and tongs and bellows. A set of jeweler's tools for the fine work. And her notes. All her notes, and sketches, and diagrams. Books' and books' worth.

Catanape's bed and Sharpear's perch. Nosebloom's favorite toy. And Jackheart's hoard, small shiny bright items he had collected over the past two years. Jackheart was her first mechanico and her dearest, but Jacqueline spent three precious hours returning other students' belongings that the crow had stolen.

Jacqueline left the campus with just an hour to spare. The mule, a spavined old creature that gave lie to the University's generosity, wasn't happy with the setting sun. He knew he belonged in his stable, eating sweet oats in his dotage, not being hitched to an ramshackle cart and trekking for who knew how long.

Jacqueline added a mechanico beast of burden to her long list of planned projects.

Nosebloom nipped at the mule's hooves, dodging halfhearted kicks with yipping aplomb. Catanape stretched, letting her claws extend, from atop her leather cushion. Jackheart, as always, perched on her shoulder. Sharpears, not yet switched on, was wrapped in soft wool blankets and stored in a bag. Jacqueline had installed the power sources, but hadn't completed the final connections.

The University was located an hour west of the capital city. Home was to the east, where her parents could rail at her for failing.

Jacqueline intended to continue west with the setting sun.

———

JACQUELINE WALKED beside the cart til the moon rose and set.

Nosebloom had long past jumped up into the cart and nestled next to Catanape, despite the latter's hiss of annoyance.

Wealthy folk had the new steam powered vehicles, but off the main roads, the world favored travel afoot. Jacqueline had passed through the small town that supported the University, but there was nothing after that, except for the occasional farmstead cleared out from the oaken forest.

Least not that she could reach with the old mule's pace in the few hours she wanted to travel.

She'd turned off the main road an hour ago, just hoping to find a suitable spot to camp. Space to rent in a farmer's barn. Anything.

She was tired, so tired, when they crested the next hill, the road narrowed to a rocky dirt path.

And there it was. A compound, dilapidated in the starlight. Falling down weathered wood fence, tall feathery weeds grown up around the gate post, ramshackle wooden buildings with blistered white paint in the dim light. A monastery? Some order of recluses tucked deep in the woods, long since gone? Jacqueline didn't know and didn't care this late at night, with her feet blistered and the mule half lame.

She smelled dust and wood rot as she passed through the creaking wooden gate, and an underlying unpleasant musk.

The mule planted his hooves.

"Come on, come on," Jacqueline said, her voice loud in the hush. No insects, no frogs, no night calling birds. She knew it, the mule knew it, something was wrong, but Jacqueline couldn't go on. She just couldn't. Not for tonight.

Fine. She'd tether the mule just outside the gate with a bucket of water and a flake of hay. Her tools and books would be safe, in the cart. The mechanicos would come with her.

She unhitched, fed, and watered the mule, then woke the mechanicos.

"Come, my lovelies," she murmured. The mechanicos, except for dormant Sharpears, whirled to life. Catanape and Nosebloom stretched, gears creaking in the cold night air. Jackheart spread his wings and flapped.

Jacqueline entered the largest building, a raw magelight burning painlessly in her palm. The building, a wooden structure two stories tall, was filled with dusty tables and broken benches and molding bookshelves. Part of the wooden ceiling had collapsed, letting the cold starlight in. Shadows crept along the edges of the walls and bookshelves.

Jacqueline shivered. *Avoid the large spaces.* This wasn't really what the Dean had meant, but the advice applied regardless. She backed out before a shadow could touch her, closing her fingers over the magelight.

"Let's try the building adjacent," she said to Jackheart.

He quorked and rubbed his bronze bill against her cheek.

The building to the left looked to be the remainder of the kitchen. A similar hole in the roof allowed light, enough starlight for Jacqueline to feel uneasy in this space, too. The kitchen was spacious enough to feed fifty or more people, with multiple stoves and fireplaces lining the walls, and four long wooden tables filling the center of the room.

But off to the right was a door that, once opened, revealed a pantry, six feet square, empty but for a couple sacks of moldy flour. Jacqueline set the magelight on a shelf and hauled the flour sacks out to the center of the kitchen.

She could stay in here for the night. Leave first thing in the morning.

She dug out some cheese and a heel of bread and a steel canteen of fresh water. She didn't trust anything from the kitchen, not even water out of the pipes. Nosebloom and Catanape paced back and forth in front of the door. The magelight was just enough to illuminate the pantry, the mechanicos, Jacqueline's bedding...and Sharpear's bag.

Now that Jacqueline had stopped walking, her brain sped up. She couldn't sleep, not yet. And all Sharpears needed to live was about a half hour of focused work.

She unpacked the owl and her fine jeweler's tools and linked the power source to the mechanico's body, each copper wire twisted just so, soldered *there* and *there*. The gem that processed the sunlight and moonlight glowed once she completed the last connection. The owl twisted her head around to gaze at Jacqueline with the smooth whir of lubricated gears, the large orange eyes glowing in the dim pantry. She hooted, a fluting call, soft for a creature so fierce.

"Sharpears," said Jacqueline. "You are Sharpears, born to hunt the night."

The owl twisted her head back towards the door, her hoots questioning. Catanape and Nosebloom stopped pacing and glanced at Jacqueline as well. Catanape yowled, as demanding as any flesh and blood cat. And Nosebloom, usually the sweetest of dogs, growled at the door.

*Stay to the small.*

"I don't want to risk you," Jacqueline said. Even the kitchen was big. Big enough for something evil to claim, for something evil to hunt within.

*It's our choice, mama,* each seemed to say, Sharpears newly born, Catanape fierce, Nosebloom protective. *We are meant to guard. To protect. Let us do our duty.*

Jackheart nestled against her. *I love you but I'm staying right here. I'm a day flyer and a scrounger and a trickster.*

Nosebloom scratched at the door.

Jacqueline opened the door, ignoring the brief stab of guilt as she did so. The mechanicos slipped out into the star-dim darkness, their eyes glowing. Jackheart pulled the door shut with his beak then snuggled back against Jacqueline.

And somehow, Jacqueline slept.

———

*BLOOD AND RAGE AND DARKNESS!* Jacqueline screamed herself awake, with no distinct memory of the nightmares that woke her. *Blood and hunger!*

Jackheart quorked softly from the doorway.

Jacqueline grabbed a hammer. She had no other weapons. But she had to check on her menagerie.

The kitchen floor was coated with blood, dark in the predawn light filtering through the broken ceiling.

And in the center of the kitchen, between two of the tables, the flour sacks burst, lay a huge demon rat, bigger than a person.

Not moving. Its body bore tears and bites and rips. The work of her owl, her cat, and her spaniel—each of whom lay beyond the demon rat.

Jacqueline rushed to them. Sharpears blinked her great orange eyes. One wing was askew, and the talons on the opposite foot had been wrenched and bent. But her power source was intact. She would survive.

Catanape was similarly injured, a cracked canine tooth gleaming in the gray light. Her eyes glowed green, and she purred, the rumbling creak of gears in her chest vibrating.

And Nosebloom? He wagged his stump of a tail, and stood up, his right front paw held up, and limped to her, nudging her with his cold metal nose.

Okay. They would all be okay.

Jackheart screeched behind her, a sound of fury and fear she'd never heard from him before. She spun around.

The demon rat now crouched, black eyes gleaming with malice, Jackheart trapped between its long yellow incisors.

The rat crunched down. And spat out Jackheart's crumpled body.

*Her heart.*

Jacqueline howled and leaped for the rat, beating it with the hammer, powered by muscles forged from years of metalwork. The rat gnashed at her with its sharp teeth, ripping into her other arm even as she hit its skull with the hammer.

She'd never purposefully hurt any creature before in her life.

But now she did, beating it until its skull cracked and its eyes bulged out and blood and brain matter splattered her face and that awful keening stopped.

*Her* keening. The demon rat was silent. Truly dead, now, not just feigning.

*Oh, Jackheart.* She collapsed to her knees next to his mangled mechanico body. Picked him up and cradled him. The rat had twisted and torn one wing. But worse, the rat had pierced Jackheart's chest, containing his precious power source.

She sobbed, letting her tears flood over his body.

*Quork?*

Soft, so soft. Had she imagined it?

Jacqueline lifted Jackheart's body to her ear. A gear clicked, then another. And another.

*Quork.* He opened his eyes, the obsidian blackness softly glowing in the morning light.

*Quork!*

———

THE MULE WAS FINE. Likely someone, somehow, had magically chained the demon to the monastery's grounds, and the mule was *outside.*

Of course, that just meant the mule had more sense than her.

With the death of the demon rat, the unsettling muskiness had dissipated.

Jacqueline entered the main building. In daylight, she could see the remnants of the past battle. Bones, human bones, cracked and gnawed, were piled under the tables and against the shelves.

She didn't think she could bury all of them. But she knew how to make a fire hot enough to forge steel. And that would burn the bones.

And let her mend her brave mechanicos.

Jacqueline set to work.

# BLOOD TRACKS

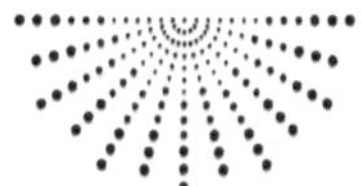

The train car was empty. Lingering scents of cologne and perfume hearkened to recent passengers, but no one remained in this car. Late afternoon, the trains weren't as busy. That would change soon as it grew closer to the end of the day.

Bettina limped to the closest seat, tossed her ragged green and pink canvas backpack onto the adjacent seat, and settled, panting, her wet jeans squelching against the stained and scratched plastic, her thin shoulders hunched, her bruised hands clenched in front of her.

She watched the platform anxiously through her long dark bangs as she caught her breath.

It remained empty.

She let herself relax as soon as the train started moving, the electric hum of the tracks a calming white noise. She would have at least ten minutes of respite, until the next stop.

Her hands ached. The fingernail on her left thumb was torn down to the quick, with just a millimeter of the ripped bit of nail attached.

She yanked it off with her teeth, savoring the coppery flecks of dried blood. Not hers. She could taste the bloodlines and the inherent power of her assailant, and reckoned herself lucky to have broken free. Badger. They didn't let go easily. She had scraped and bruised her hands against the iron cuff around his right wrist, freeing herself.

She carefully placed the bit of nail deep in her front pocket, the damp tightness of the denim applying brief pressure against the pulsing throb of her abused nail bed, then leaned back against the seat. The adjacent window was open about an inch, letting in drips of rain and cold air that flattened her damp, torn t-shirt against her breasts and rib cage. She shivered, but she was too tired to reach up to close the window.

Anyways, the cold would keep her alert. She was clever, sneaky, and fast. That had saved her long enough for her to get on this train.

But with her hurt ankle, fast may not be possible right now, even if she wasn't bone tired. She didn't think it was broken, but only her sturdy leather combat boots, laces cinched tight, kept her ankle from swelling into a cantaloupe.

And sneaky was definitely out. Even if they didn't know which particular train she was on, they were aware of her. Awareness was the antithesis of sneakiness.

That left clever, and she had to be alert to be clever. Cold sharpened her. Fear sharpened her.

Her gaze flickered around the train car. Bright digital ads ran along the sides of the train above the windows. PSAs about courteous train travel, a commercial for a personal injury lawyer, and a series of "Have You Seen This Person" photos.

No photo of her. Yet.

The train entered the tunnels, swapping the pallid late afternoon sky for intermittent flashes of yellow lights.

*Meat.* She could smell it. She noted a brown paper lunch bag, top crumpled to keep it closed, on the seat kitty corner to her, and her stomach growled.

She hadn't eaten since yesterday. Hunger might sharpen her, but it also weakened her. She reached for the support pole in the center of the aisle, keeping as much pressure off her ankle as possible, and stretched for the bag.

It had a hopeful weightiness to it. She collapsed back into her seat and opened it. Inside was a crumpled napkin, an opened, rolled up foil packet of mayo, and, yes, half of a sandwich, rare roast beef and dark red tomatoes and rich mayonnaise oozing along the corner, that was only missing a couple bites.

She chomped into it, tasting the impressions of grass and hills and sunlight still remaining after cooking the meat. Real cow, not vat grown beef. Grass-fed. Fancy. A life as ephemeral as the now-eaten sandwich, digesting in her tummy.

Only people with enough money to buy a sandwich like that didn't care if they left it behind.

Five more minutes to the next station. Five more minutes to see if she could get just a little further away. Maybe even make it to the safe house she'd heard of, off River Street.

Maybe even escape.

She hadn't heard from Mama yet. A week, and no word. When Mama had promised to text as soon as she'd reached the border, then again when she reached La Paz.

Her assailant was a badger: tenacious, fierce, often tasked with bringing people in, in one piece. Gifted with strength and single-minded focus. Kind of boring, and common, but they had their uses in all sorts of organizations.

Her gifts differed. She could tell, just from the taste of flake of dried blood or a morsel flesh, everything about the skills of the creature from which they came.

But she had *more*, which is why the Unity Corporation wanted her. She could sense and identify, with just a whiff of scent, no matter how far away.

She'd never heard of anyone who could do *that*. Sense from afar. Made her special.

Days like this, she could do without special.

She could only sense within a quarter mile, maybe a half on a day where she was full and rested. So she had no idea who or what waited for her, if anyone did, at the next stop.

She licked her fingers, getting all the juices from the tomatoes and beef. All the crumbs of bread. She sucked on the mayo package.

Jiggled out the last of the crumbs left in the bag, then put the mayo package into it, crumpled it all up, and shoved it into her backpack. No point leaving any saliva behind.

Her cell vibrated from within her backpack. No time to dig it out. It might be Mama, calling from Mexico, but if that was the case, she could call her back.

And Mama had said she wouldn't call. Just text.

Maybe it wasn't Mama.

But she couldn't get rid of the phone yet.

Two minutes.

Badger, rhino, hawk? She couldn't sense anyone with talent ahead of her.

One minute.

Still nothing.

*Next stop Mercy Street Station Next stop Mercy Street Station Next stop Mercy Street Station*

She hauled herself up and limped towards the door, grasping the vertical steel poles as the train slowed. The last lurch had her sucking in a yelp of pain, then the door opened and she had to just jump down onto the stained concrete and brick platform, dodge the few norms waiting to board the train, and head towards the maintenance tunnels.

A songbird busked in the center of the platform, taking advantage of the acoustics in the station, a paper coffee cup stuffed full of dollar bills on the floor in front of her. Her clear voice took flight, pulling nearby travelers to her.

Bettina resisted the temptation to stop, to listen, and hobbled past. The songbird, a slender black girl in an orange and brown vintage caftan, winked at her. Sang louder, lifting her arms like wings.

*Date prisa*, hurry hurry, and what wouldn't she give for the speed of a cheetah, the stealth of a jaguar, even the camouflage of chameleon if she couldn't be big and fierce, all hundred and ten pounds of her dripping wet with blood if she was caught. She snaked through the small crowd towards the metal door at the near end of the station wall, muttering apologies as she jostled past.

Most of the norms didn't even notice the skinny brown girl.

Her senses flared as she yanked on the maintenance door, its rusted squeal stabbing her ears.

*HAWK!*

The door wedged partway open, caught on a crack in the platform.

A shrill scream echoed off the pitted marbled arch of the Mercy Station ceiling. The hawk, a tall white woman dressed in a Unity Corporation uniform, wearing the typical iron cuff tight against her right wrist, had seen her.

Bettina squeezed through the doorway, tugging to close the door behind her. The door, still hopelessly snagged on that crack, didn't budge, so she lurched into the darkness, tripping over debris as she focused, *sensing*.

Just the hawk on the platform.

And she didn't think the hawk would follow into the darkness. Not when it couldn't see the creatures that lurked within.

Lucky again. Lucky there was no owl. Unity Corp usually sent the birds out in pairs.

She slowed to a walk. She didn't know how long she could keep running, keep hiding. Her ankle hurt like crazy and she just wanted to sleep. To go home.

Home was gone. The minute her senior class came up for the random blood test, her life masquerading as a norm, taking Advanced Placement classes, winning swim meets, was over.

The tunnel was lit by dim yellow emergency lights, spaced every ten yards or so. Which would be fine except more of the lights were broken, than working, leaving deep patches of darkness in between.

The air tasted of moist decay and rat urine and dry scales, the scents swirling around her like the wake of a speeding train.

"Are you lost, little girl?"

She stiffened, then limped faster, stifling a sob.

*Lost lost lost* echoed against the dripping walls. Footsteps followed her.

If she continued straight, the next station was Alpha Avenue. Servicing the headquarters of the Unity Corporation.

She needed to take the tunnel branch that led to the River Street station of the Blue Line. She could see the next flickering light, twenty yards ahead. That should be it.

"Are you lost?" the dry reptilian voice repeated.

*Lost lost lost*

"No," she said, her voice swallowed by the damp. No fear. Show no fear. But she could smell the stink of her own fear wafting off of her. An enticing as pheromones to the creatures who lived in the tunnels.

She just had to be brave a little bit longer. Ignore the taps of claws on concrete behind her. Ten yards to the side passageway. Five.

"The River Street safe house was raided this morning. If that's where you're going."

She stopped and turned to face the gator.

He was a young teenager, green scales pocking his pale cheeks like colorblind acne. His pupils were slivers in his amber eyes, narrowed against the yellow light. He wore baggy jeans and a loose t-shirt. A combat belt around his waist held several pouches and canteens. A flashlight on a carabiner clip dangled from a belt loop.

His scaled, clawed feet were bare.

Sometimes the nanos gave more than just mental abilities and heightened senses.

She could pass for a norm. He couldn't.

His right wrist ended in a stump.

"Most everyone got away," he said. "I stayed in the tunnels to warn anyone trying to reach the safe house." He smiled, a sharp tooth scraping his lower lip.

Not reassuring.

"I need a place to hide," she said. For all his scrawniness, he looked strong. She didn't know if she could trust him, but pretending might buy her time. "That's why I was trying to reach the safe house."

He detached the flashlight and handed it to her.

"What are you?" he asked, gesturing with his stump for her to follow. He turned right at the junction, away from the route to the River Street Station.

"Hound," Bettina said.

He glanced back at her. "That can't be it," he said, voice skeptical. "There's way too much action for just a hound who slipped her leash."

She bristled. "I've never been leashed."

"Lucky you," he said. "What are you?"

"If I focus, I can feel who's around me."

"I can *see* who's around me. How far?"

"At least a quarter mile," she admitted.

He frowned. That was worse than his smile. "Neat, but...."

She shrugged. "Not mine to ask why. Just trying to stay out of reach. Avoid the leash. Collar. Whatever." She snuck a peek at his stump. Long healed.

"Chewed my hand off," he said, catching her. "Two years ago. I was just a kid, but I knew I didn't want to be Unity's soldier for rent."

Just a kid? He was all of what, fifteen?

At thirteen, she was still in school, trying to decide if she wanted to be a doctor or engineer. Or both. Before the nanobytes that had escaped a decade ago, and infested everyone, changed her.

Most people had been affected right away, when the nanobytes escaped. The few babies still being born came out of the womb manifesting powers. Or not. For most people, nothing seemed to change. Maybe a better immune system. Maybe not. The nanos just coexisted. Doing whatever nanos do.

For a few people, though, the changes made them ... different. Markedly different. And the later the changes occurred, the more striking the powers.

People who manifested were involuntarily employed by Unity Corporation, sanctioned by the government. Normal people didn't want the freaks running around using their powers unfettered. Some slipped through. Songbirds and the like. The ones the norms thought were helpless, or pretty.

She'd thought she was a norm. Until that morning, two years ago, when she was eating contraband bacon, and she *saw* the pigs in their tiny enclosures, waiting for the bolt guns they couldn't escape.

She hadn't told anyone except her mama.

Kids were tested yearly until junior high, then testing became unannounced and random.

Her senior class at her high school got lucky. Or not. Not for her.

She could *feel* the hounds entering the school compound. Approaching the wing that included her classroom.

Saw her physics teacher Mr Reed answer a call from the front office in the middle of the *Acceleration Due to Gravity* lab. Saw nod, hang up, and stare at his students. At Bettina.

She abandoned her lab partner, marched right up to Mr Reed's desk at the front of the room.

"I gotta leave," she told him. She shifted her weight back and forth. "I'm really sorry, Mr Reed, but I have to go. Now."

"Bettina—"

"Please, Mr Reed." She was his best student, she knew she was. He *knew* she wouldn't ask something unauthorized unless the need was dire.

She hoped so, anyways.

"The blood test—"

"Please!"

He'd nodded, took out his key ring, separated an old-fashioned key from the chip keys. "This will get you out without setting off any alarms. Good luck."

She'd taken it and ran. Used it on the gate near the teacher's parking lot. Threw the key into the river. Didn't even try to go home, though she called Mama and left the message they'd prearranged: *Bettina was skipping swim practice that afternoon.*

Mama would have left right then, run all the way to La Paz and Tia Claudia. Wait for Bettina there, in Tia Claudia's house overlooking the Sea of Cortez.

That was the plan.

She didn't know if Mama had made it to La Paz. Didn't know if she'd even made it out of the city.

Bettina didn't know what happened to Mr Reed, either. If anyone found out he helped her.

That was a week ago. She'd been stuck in the city ever since.

"Where are we going?" she asked the gator. They'd passed multiple junctions. She was hopelessly lost, for real. Her ankle had gone numb. Her flashlight beam was dimming.

"Not too much farther," he said, then stopped at a small, rusted door. "Here we are."

He tapped on it, a quick sequence, then knocked again. The door creaked partway open, revealing the smooth iridescent face of a small woman, squinting in the fading beam of the flashlight.

"Found one," he said, pulling Bettina in front of him. "Hound. Maybe she'll help us."

"Help you? I have to get out of here," Bettina said.

"Help us, we'll help you," the woman said, her voice soft. "Nothing's free."

She could be in her thirties or fifties. Bettina couldn't tell. Her features were delicate, her hair shiny black streaked with gray. Thick scars encircled her right wrist.

"She'd be a good guard," the gator continued. "Or lookout. Said she could sense powers within a quarter mile."

"Gee, thanks," Bettina said. Years she'd guarded her secret, and now the first person she'd told was blabbing it.

"Ah. Saw her on the newsfeed. She doesn't look all that dangerous. Come in, child." The woman stepped aside.

"See ya later," the boy said, smirking, as Bettina squeezed through the door. He saluted with his stump, then trotted off, claws snicking on the damp concrete floor.

This passageway, running parallel to the regular maintenance tunnel, was tighter, and she had to duck if she didn't want to scrape the top of her head on the ceiling. She stepped over one of the large cables snaking along the ceiling and floor. The cables left only a narrow space in the center to stoop along. But it was dry, and didn't smell of rat urine.

"They caught a couple of our people," the woman said. "Right now they're still in holding. We're going to get them out tonight."

"I have no idea what you're talking about."

"Unity processes people through holding before transferring the ones they want to keep to their main facility."

"What about the other people?"

"Some get released."

*Some.* Bettina didn't want to ask. Didn't need to. Everyone knew someone who'd disappeared over the years. "Do I have a choice?" she asked.

"If you want our help? Sorry, but no. Nothing's free."

Bettina sensed, strained, pushed. Nothing. Nothing except the touch of an impervious shell, stretching around and behind the woman with her pale rainbow cheeks.

"What are you?" she asked.

"Child, you'll learn that's rude. But I am an oyster."

"He told you about me."

The woman sighed. "His name is Alec. Mine is Pearl. He gave me information I required. You do not need to know the powers of everyone here until I determine you do. Follow me, please."

Pearl led her to a dimly lit room, stuffed with generators, cables, and other electronics. About a half dozen people were tucked away in between the machines, chatting, snacking, resting. They fell quiet when Pearl and Bettina entered.

"A way station," Pearl said. "All automated, now, so few people even remember places like this. Safe enough for us, for a brief time."

"This is it? All the people you have to break into the Unity Corporation?" Bettina was just a high school student, but the Corporation *owned* the city. Even she knew that.

"They took two of ours. Kids. Killed three others. We have to try to get them. You help us, I'll get you out of here." Pearl called to one of the other woman sitting nearby. "Jay, do you have some extra food you can scrounge up for our friend Bettina? She's a hound. She's going to help us."

Bettina scowled. She didn't seem to have a choice, did she?

———

JAY, a plump brunette woman just a few years older than Bettina, gave her a peanut butter and strawberry sandwich. Smooth peanut butter, and Bettina preferred crunchy, but right now she didn't care. It tasted good, sweet and thick and sticking to the roof of her mouth. The carton of plain soy milk Jay handed over was the best thing she'd drank in a week.

"They got my kid sister in the raid this morning," Jay said. "Unity Corporation conscripted my older brother five years ago. Rhino. He died in Tehran on a raid. I swore I'd keep Millie safe."

"What about your parents?" Bettina didn't want to ask, but she couldn't help herself.

"Dead. After Theo died, they lost it."

"My mama should be in Mexico by now," Bettina said.

"She left you?" Jay asked, shocked.

"I ran from a blood test at school. Minute they found out I'd run, they'd be watching her. I wanted her gone before then. We both figured our chances were better on our own."

Jay pursed her lips. "Cold. But smart."

Bettina shrugged. "My plan. Mama's a norm. I'm almost eighteen. She feels I'm an adult and can make my own decisions." She dug out her phone, checked for messages. Nada.

She stretched her sense, delicately, not sure if someone on the receiving end could feel it.

Jay didn't react. Bettina inhaled, drawing in her scent. Bear. Jay was a bear. No wonder she was taking care of her kid sister. She'd be good in a fight, too.

What else? Now that she was with the others, in the way station, she could sense them. She was inside Pearl's shell, rather than outside it. Two more bears, both male. A rhino. A tiger. Thank god, something a bit more stealthy than the others. An owl. And a ferret.

"Done checking us out?" Jay asked. She waved her hand. "No techy shit needed. I could just tell by the look on your face, you weren't quite here."

"Is there really a plan?"

Jay shrugged. "Pearl has smuggled folks out of the Corporation in the past. Not often, because every time she does, they close up that route."

"How does she even know how to get in?"

Jay snorted. "She was their head of Security until five years ago.'

————

THE PLAN WAS SIMPLE. Take the tunnel to a cable intersection point that serviced the Corporation's communications. Let Pearl use up one more physical back door she'd built to get into the holding area.

The ferret would keep the security system offline, using Pearl's system back doors. Bettina would watch out for anyone getting close, the bears would collect the captured kids, then the owl would lead the kids back to the way station. The rhino, a big burly man named Crake, and the tiger, a tall lean older woman named Bonny, were simply back up muscle.

The holding area was above ground, adjacent to the main head-quarters building. Built of concrete blocks, it was a utilitarian, ugly building. Bettina had passed it daily on her way to school.

Apparently it had a musty basement filled with old equipment.

And a junction for the communications equipment, enlarged just enough for them all to squeeze through.

"Where are the guards?" Bettina asked. She couldn't sense anyone besides their group. Would Unity really use norms as guards?

"Friends," Pearl muttered. "On a coffee break. This is it. Last time in. I've used all my goodwill up."

The ferret, George, worked on an uplink to the security system, baring his teeth in frustration as he hardwired his tablet into the myriad of wires Pearl pointed out to him. Finally he slumped in relief. "Got it. Code?"

"Free at last," Pearl said.

"No one ever guessed?" Bettina snorted.

"No," Pearl said.

"Holy shit. Wow, you can do anything with that code," he said, staring at his screen, then typing madly. "Holding cells unlocked. Pearl, I think I can get into the main building."

Pearl directed the bears upstairs to free the kids; the rhino, Keven, accompanied them. A few minutes later, they led the kids back downstairs. One child, a boy, looked about eight years old; the other, a small blonde girl, about twelve, must be Millie.

"I'm sensing someone," said Bettina from the base of the stairs, stepping aside to let the bears and kids pass. "I think from the main building. Rhino. Make that two. Three."

Something felt wrong. Not rhinos. Meaner. *Hippos.*

"Hippos," she said. "Not rhinos."

"Just a matter of time," Pearl said. "George, open it up. All of it."

He stared at Pearl, wide-eyed, then nodded, punching a more keys. "Done."

Jay stopped. "Pearl, what—"

"They deserve a chance," Pearl said.

"Some of them are crazy, you told us so. Said they'd tear the city apart. All of us. Said the only safe place for them was Unity."

The other two bears guided the boy into the tunnel. The owl, Candace, led them away. George followed, yanking his tablet from the wires.

"Jay," Pearl said. "Take Millie into the tunnel."

"That's it. I'm taking my chances with the Corporation," Jay growled, sheltering Millie, a small blonde girl dressed in jeans and a t-shirt, in her arms.

"Jay," Pearl said, holding out her hand. "Jay, you have no idea what they will do with someone like Millie. I know. Trust me, even if you cooperate with them, it's not going to end well."

"Hippos are close," Bettina said. "Really close."

Jay shook her head. "Not running anymore. The city is going to burn, with what you just did. At least Unity has the infrastructure to keep us safe."

"Pearl, they're nearly here," Bettina said. Or thought she said. No one looked at her.

"Jay, this corporation is going to fall first. There's no safety here, even with Millie as a bargaining chip. Come with us, and you can turn yourselves in later, if there's anything left."

"PEARL!"

An answering roar from the top of the stairs.

"That's it," Bonny said. She pushed Jay and Millie toward the tunnel. "Go, you idiot. Get to safety now, and worry about betraying us all later."

Jay looked like she wanted to rip out Bonny's throat, but the tiger just stared back calmly. "Go. Or all our deaths will be on you. Millie's, too."

Millie and Jay scrambled through the tunnels. Bonny followed.

"Bettina, go," Pearl said. "I can close the door. Follow Bonny's orders."

"What do you mean, close the door?"

"Bonny will get you out. Trust her."

The hippos thundered down the stairs, bellowing. Unthinking. Enraged. A hound followed, stepping delicately.

Pearl stood at the base of the stairs, a tiny figure with clenched fists, the scar on right wrist shining in the dim light of the basement.

"I'm not leaving you," Bettina said.

"Hounds are loyal," Pearl said.

"I'm not a hound. But you knew that."

Pearl nodded. "I did. The water flows through both of us, my dear. Do you really want to do this?"

"I'm tired of running, too. But that doesn't mean I'm giving up." Bettina gently pushed Pearl behind her. "Go. I'll be there in a minute."

She wasn't a hound. Everyone assumed she was. But she wasn't.

She was a *shark*.

A freakin' great white.

Death from below.

———

BETTINA SQUEEZED PAST THE CABLES, arranging them just so behind her, though it didn't matter. From the noise outside, penetrating even down into the basement, everyone was too busy to hunt for them.

The hippos were dead, little pieces scattered over the floor. The hound had tried to flee. Tried. Got up to the landing before Bettina caught her.

Death from below, veridad.

Arranging the cables calmed her.

Brought her back to human.

Made her wish she could rinse the blood out of her mouth, rather than drink it down.

Pushed back her longing for the sea. She'd get there, soon enough. Baja beckoned. She dug her phone out of her back pocket. She didn't know how long comms would be up. Best to text now. **SOON**, she typed. **GOT A WAY OUT**.

Then backspaced over the message.

She didn't know if Mama was in La Paz. Or even if mama was, would there be anything else there for Bettina?

She didn't even know if Mama made it out of the city.

She caught up with Pearl at the first junction.

"We could use you here," Pearl said, like Bettina hadn't just slaughtered three large men and a woman.

"I know," Bettina said. "I think I'll stick around. Just for a bit."

She licked the last bit of blood off her teeth. She had hunting to do.

For Mama.

And for the people who would steal their lives.

# BONUS FOR THE KALEIDOSCOPE JAGUAR

*I originally started the Kaleidoscope Jaguar story much earlier in the timeline —til I realized that I was, to paraphrase what writers say, having Jacie drive to the story.*
*But I still think you can get some fun details from this. Enjoy!*

Jacie surveyed the various items laid out on the green wool Army blanket on her neatly made twin bed. She ran through her checklist. Miniature air rifle with a case full of darts: check. Three bottles of potent tranquilizers, carefully packed in bubble wrap: check. Multi-tool, including screwdrivers in Metric, English, and Mexicatl, and other nifty attachments, her own design: check.

She was wearing her Army issue jungle boots, khaki and green old school camo pants that hung loosely on her tall lanky frame, sports bra, and a close-fitting black t-shirt. Comfortable enough to nap in, sturdy enough for fieldwork. She tossed a couple extra pair of green wool socks and quick dry fabric bikini underwear onto the pile, then added an additional sports bra and t-shirt. One more pair of khaki pants; a lightweight chambray button down that would serve to keep off burning sunlight as well as voracious insects; and a floppy-brimmed canvas hat that still smelled of citronella.

A couple rechargeable anti-insect charms on fine silver chains to be worn as necklaces; a dozen smooth tumbled smoky quartz pebbles, water purification charms to be dropped into water bottles as needed; three these-aren't-the-droids charms, inch-wide iron-studded leather straps that could be worn as bracelets; and a doeskin pouch of gold Mexicatl coinage.

Anything else she needed she could purchase in Ciudad Ojinaja de los Rios in Mexicatl, four worlds away.

Including a mule, a cart and a whomping big crate for the kaleidoscope jaguar cub Montrose was paying her to collect.

————

SHE DIDN'T KNOW SPECIFICALLY how Deanna Montrose of Dallas, Texas had found her.

That was normal. Clients found her by quiet word of mouth: from offball Reddit threads, from dark web chat rooms, from surreptitious chitchat at fundraisers held by American old money royalty.

Jacie was a low level sorceress with an inborn talent for world crossing and a knack for trouble. She funneled her skills and propensity into a career as a magical Indiana Jones via Steve Irwin, visiting nearby worlds and, for a price (a very, very good price), collecting critters.

A month ago, Montrose had emailed her. She wanted a jaguar cub, but not just a normal Panthera onca from Central America. She wanted something truly unique; at least, unique to this Earth.

Montrose had somehow heard of the kaleidoscope jaguars of Mexicatl. And she wanted one.

At that, Jacie nicknamed Montrose 'Veruka', but accepted, after laying out her own terms.

No trophy hunts. No endangered species. Natural living arrangements, top notch veterinary care, and appropriate husbandry, with Jacie to verify periodically at the client's expense.

Montrose agreed.

———

AN AIRLINE roared overhead as she tossed her high tech carbon-fiber-framed, fully loaded backpack into the trunk of her vintage charcoal gray Alfa Romeo Spider convertible.

It would be at least a fifteen hour drive. Flying might be faster, with Los Angles International only ten minutes from her Spanish bungalow in El Segundo, but she preferred the freedom of driving.

The black ragtop was up and latched. The drive from Los Angeles to Marfa, Texas would be a hot one, even in September. Last time she'd made the mistake of a long daytime drive with the top down she'd paid for it with burnt skin and a headache that went on for days.

The top came down, though, when the sun set, six hours later.

She was well into the Sonoran desert by then, Kyuss and other desert rock blasting through her speakers via the cassette smart phone adapter. The Milky Way glittered above her in the dark velvety sky.

She switched her musical options to Latin hip hop once she got to New Mexico and the Chihuahuan desert. Music helped her focus. And it kept her awake on the long drive, so she could review the upcoming operation.

The Earth that included Mexicatl was wetter and warmer than her Earth. That Earth had a bit less tilt than hers, less variance in seasons. Once she crossed from Ojinaga, here, to Cuidad Ojinaja de los Rios, there, she'd go from stark desert to lush jungle, jungle that she'd never before explored.

Fun!

She wouldn't be alone. Dani Blackblood would be joining her in Marfa. A semi-retired veterinary anesthesiologist who lived in Austin, Texas, she was Jacie's ace in the hole for getting the sedated jaguar safely delivered.

Dani had helped on trips in the past, safely sedating critters from baby triceratop-like dinos (that big meteor missed Mexicatl's earth, though volcanoes still super-erupted), to dire wolf pups from way up north in Kanata, just two worlds away and still stuck in an ice age. (Once the first season Game of Thrones came out on HBO, there was a run on dire wolf puppies. Jacie detested snow, flat out hated the cold, so she charged a premium for those pups.)

Jacie arrived in Marfa at 3 a.m. She'd rented a private, pet-friendly home on the outskirts of the artsy town for the next month. A month was probably overkill, but time differences could get a little out of whack the more worlds away you traveled.

And she didn't know how long it would take them to trap a cub. Past experience said about a week.

The single-story white painted adobe house occupied a small portion of the half acre, fenced, cacti-and-chaparral landscaped lot, set well back down a long, narrow gravel driveway. Dani's silver SUV was already parked in front of the house, glinting in the moonlight. Jacie parked the Alfa behind to it, grabbed her backpack, keyed in the code on the front door, then entered the house as quietly as she could.

Which, for a low level sorceress, was pretty darn quiet.

She still woke Dani up. By the time Jacie had plopped her back-pack next to the queen-sized bed in her room (Dani had left the door open, and a nightlight on in the attached bath), Dani was in her door-way, sturdy short form clothed in a snug Rocket Raccoon orange tank and baggy charcoal gray flannel pajama bottoms. Her short brown and silver pixie haircut was tousled, her green eyes sleepy behind thick glasses. "Hey, kiddo," she said, her throaty voice thick with sleep, drawing Jacie in for a quick hug then, standing up on her tiptoes, a kiss on Jacie's cheek. "How was the drive?"

"Uneventful. My favorite," Jacie said. "Yours?"

"Ditto. Got pulled over once, but the cop was ex Army, and he saw my West Point decal. Let me off with a warning." Dani was a speed demon, albeit with utmost control. "I'm back to bed. Nine a.m. okay for breakfast? I got some eggs and stuff when I got in yesterday. Everything shuts down on Sunday in Marfa, so we don't have any other options for later."

"Sounds great. Thanks for doing that. 'Night." Jacie shut her door, stripped, then slipped under the cream colored, fluffy down comforter on her bed.

Her last thoughts were of gamboling rainbow kittens, pouncing among the stars of the Milky Way, chasing meteors like they were the dots of light from laser pointers.

———

AFTER EGGS and toast and coffee, lots of coffee, Jacie and Dani loaded up their gear in Dani's SUV for the drive to Presidio.

Ojinaga was just across the border in Mexico. The crossing to Ciudad Ojinaja de los Rios, Mexicatl, was near an old Spanish Revival style church, Parroquia de Jesus Nazareno.

They left Dani's vehicle in Roberto's Auto Shop and Garage in Presidio. Roberto would keep the SUV safe, and likely change oil and detail the interior before they got back. Two years ago, Roberto's daughter Gabi had been abducted, and taken a world away. Jacie had recovered her.

The kidnappers would never steal anyone's child away again.

They walked into the modern border crossing building adjacent to the car entry point with its new arched shade. With a quick press of iron into her flesh, drawing just a spot of blood, Jacie deployed one of the these-aren't-the-droids charms she was wearing as a bracelet on her right wrist. She couldn't risk the rifle and tranquilizers being confiscated, and all the associated trouble that would bring. As well as the time delay.

The border agent, a trim, clean shaven man in a neatly pressed khaki uniform, reviewed Dani's passport and waved her past with a quick smile.

That smile faded to a scowl when he met Jacie's eyes.

" Buenos días, senor. ¿Cómo está?" Jacie said, gritting her teeth and pressing the iron spur deeper into her arm. Just her luck -- the man must be sensitive. Rather than making him not worry about her pack, the charm triggered his attention.

And attention meant suspicion on the border.

"Open your pack, senorita," he said, gesturing to an adjacent, stainless-steel topped table.

Jacie picked up her backpack with her left hand, taking the opportunity to swing it against her right wrist as she lifted the pack to the table. The stab of pain from the iron spur ripping her outer wrist was worth the look of confusion, then concern, on the border agent's face, as a few drops of her blood splattered on the cream and gray terrazzo floor.

"Are you alright, senorita?" he said. "Please, go to the lavatory and wash up." He gestured to a bathroom beyond the checkpoint. "Move along, move along."

YES! Oh, it wasn't fair to the border agent, he'd likely have a headache for a few hours. And she hated that this world sometimes required that extra bit of sacrifice to fuel the charms. She'd once visited a world that was worse, far worse; she was missing the tip of her pinkie, because her own magic lacked the oomph to open the crossing home.

In Mexicatl, magic dripped everywhere. Problem was, Jacie's innate ability level stayed the same. So, yeah, she'd be stronger, but everything or everyone else with more magical ability was proportionally stronger than her. It was a wash.

Catching Dani's eyes, Jacie jerked her chin in the direction of the women's restroom.

———

JACIE RINSED her wrist under the faucet, hissing as the warm water hit her torn flesh.

"Dude, it needs stitches, except you turned it into hamburger that can't be stitched." Dani fished the first aid kit out of her pack. "I still have some of that healing ointment from the last trip. Should it still be good?"

"Well, the base is a triple antibiotic, so if nothing else, it has that." Jacie appreciated that, after Dani's initial disbelief, she now took the magic stuff in stride.

Dani smeared ointment on Jacie's wrist, applied a nonstick pad, then wrapped some cotton padding and gauze around her wrist, keeping the pad in place. She finished off the bandage with a layer of black, stretchy self-stick material. "There you go."

"Thanks. Now, vámonos. Time's flying. Let's go catch a kitty."

———

Parroquia de Jesus Nazareno was a small church on a flat paver-covered lot. A couple palm trees flanked the church itself. The town had placed its name, Ojinaga, in big blocky rainbow letters, across the plaza, beginning with a tall blue O and ending with a shorter violet A. No one stood by them right now, but Jacie could picture little kids climbing on them.

A red clay tiled gazebo and a small concrete, drained pool, interior painted sky blue, with a central three-tiered fountain, nestled in the space between the letters and the church. Coffee and cinnamon wafted from a nearby panadería. Short trees and wrought iron benches lined the borders of the plaza.

The crossing wasn't inside the church, for which Jacie was grateful. Her view on religion was that gods and other supernatural creatures were inhabitants of other worlds that had traveled to or fell into this world. She'd heard of Quetzalcoatl in Mexicatl, and even seen a Bigfoot in Kanata.

She respected those creatures for the power they actually held, not the power that ignorant inhabitants of this world gave them. Nonetheless, churches, especially those where people had worshiped for decades to centuries, gave her the willies. There was a magic in belief and worship, and it wasn't friendly to her.

Luckily, the crossing was via the fountain. "Ready?" she said to Dani, holding out her hand. Dani grasped it firmly, and they both stepped over the wall, and into the empty pool ...

... and through a thick mist, as Jacie focused her will ... and found themselves, retching, with warm water up to their knees, in the very definitely not drained fountain on the Ciudad Ojinaja de los Rios side.

The fountain was octagonal, not round, and more elaborate, with intensely colored, iridescent tiles in geometric pinwheels and chevrons along the three foot tall walls. Jacie could feel sweat trickling along her cropped hairline and between her breasts.

"Been awhile," she gasped, reaching for a water bottle dangling off her backpack and taking a swig before climbing out the fountain.

# ABOUT THE AUTHOR

Since graduating from West Point, Stephannie Tallent has served in the Army as a Military Intelligence officer during Desert Storm, gotten a Zoology degree, went to vet school, worked as a small animal veterinarian, and designed and published knitting patterns and books.

Throughout all that she's always wanted to be a writer, and she's finally put all her type A, soft-spoken, invisible middle-aged woman focus on that goal, writing everything from fantasy to science fiction, mysteries and romance.

She has sold stories to **Pulphouse Magazine** and the **WMG Holiday Spectacular**.

www.stephannietallent.com

Sign up for Stephannie's newsletter!
https://www.stephannietallent.com/subscribe/

# ALSO BY STEPHANNIE TALLENT

*Short Story Collections*

Gates of Wonder

The Chronicles of Dinah Lee Wright Vol 1

The Chronicles of Dinah Lee Wright Vol 2

Gratitude of the Ocean: Jolene Tomberlin Series

The Serpent in the Shallows: Jolene Tomberlin Series

The Monkey's Journal

The Kaleidoscope Jaguars of the Jungles of Mexicatl

The Mermaid of Ellis Prime

The Alchemy of Science and Mystery

One Plus One Equals More (mystery/crime)

A Snowman Made of Sand (romance)

KnitWitch (fantasy and knitting patterns)